COSCOM
ENTERTAINMENT

ALSO BY A.P. FUCHS

BLOOD OF MY WORLD TRILOGY

DISCOVERY OF DEATH
MEMORIES OF DEATH
LIFE OF DEATH

UNDEAD WORLD TRILOGY

BLOOD OF THE DEAD
POSSESSION OF THE DEAD
REDEMPTION OF THE DEAD

THE AXIOM-MAN™ SAGA
(LISTED IN READING ORDER)

AXIOM-MAN
EPISODE NO. 0: FIRST NIGHT OUT
DOORWAY OF DARKNESS
EPISODE NO. 1: THE DEAD LAND
CITY OF RUIN
EPISODE NO. 2: UNDERGROUND CRUSADE
OUTLAW
OF MAGIC AND MEN (COMIC BOOK)

OTHER FICTION

A STRANGER DEAD
A RED DARK NIGHT
APRIL (WRITING AS PETER FOX)
MAGIC MAN (DELUXE CHAPBOOK)
THE WAY OF THE FOG (THE ARK OF LIGHT VOL. 1)
DEVIL'S PLAYGROUND (WRITTEN WITH KEITH GOUVEIA)
ON HELL'S WINGS (WRITTEN WITH KEITH GOUVEIA)
ZOMBIE FIGHT NIGHT: BATTLES OF THE DEAD

MAGIC MAN PLUS 15 TALES OF TERROR
UNDENIABLE

ANTHOLOGIES (AS EDITOR)

DEAD SCIENCE
ELEMENTS OF THE FANTASTIC
VICIOUS VERSES AND REANIMATED RHYMES: ZANY ZOMBIE
POETRY FOR THE UNDEAD HEAD
METAHUMANS VS THE UNDEAD
BIGFOOT TERROR TALES VOL. 1 (WITH ERIC S. BROWN)
BIGFOOT TERROR TALES VOL. 2 (WITH ERIC S. BROWN)
METAHUMANS VS WEREWOLVES

NON-FICTION

BOOK MARKETING FOR THE
FINANCIALLY-CHALLENGED AUTHOR
CANADIAN SCRIBBLER: COLLECTED LETTERS OF AN
UNDERGROUND WRITER
LOOK, UP ON THE SCREEN! THE BIG BOOK OF
SUPERHERO MOVIE REVIEWS
GETTING DOWN AND DIGITAL: HOW TO SELF-PUBLISH
YOUR BOOK

POETRY

THE HAND I'VE BEEN DEALT
HAUNTED MELODIES AND OTHER DARK POEMS
STILL ABOUT A GIRL

GO TO

WWW.CANISTERX.COM
&
WWW.AXIOM-MAN.COM

EPISODE No. 2

Axiom-Man
UNDERGROUND
CRUSADE

by

A.P. Fuchs

COSCOM ENTERTAINMENT

WINNIPEG

ISBN 978-1-927339-49-7

Published by COSCOM ENTERTAINMENT
www.coscomentertainment.com

Check out AXIOM-MAN on the web at
www.axiom-man.com

Text set in Garamond; Printed and Bound in the USA

COVER ART BY JUSTIN SHAUF AND KYLE ZAJAC

This is for Lewis, a little mystery man
in his own right.

I love you, son.

Axiom-Man
UNDERGROUND
CRUSADE

CHAPTER ONE

GABRIEL MOVED OUT of the way when the guy seated next to him received a beer bottle to the back of his head. The guy's face went straight into the bar top. His neck craned back when a burly dude with pythons for arms pulled him to his feet by his hair.

The man who'd just been jacked with the bottle was still coming around, his eyes wildly darting around through the blood on his face, trying to see who'd just clocked him even though the guy who did was standing right next to him.

"Six times I've told you to leave Katie alone," the big guy said.

The other man wiped the blood from his face. "Katie who?" His voice trembled, but Gabriel thought it wasn't from fear, rather from still being out of it after being struck. "Look, man, this is twice you've come after me. I've done nothing. Nothing!"

The big guy slammed a meaty fist into the bloody man's stomach. The guy's legs came off the floor, folding upward from the impact. He should've bent forward, but the guy holding his head stopped that from happening. Gabriel could only imagine how much the shot hurt.

Gabriel's heart beat quickly. He was no stranger to violence and had tangled with worse than this guy as Axiom-man, but getting into a fight wasn't tonight's mission, and he wasn't sure if he should intervene and get himself noticed, especially if he decided to come back to Dave's Bar in the future. It seemed like a good place to keep one's ear to the ground and hear what was going on in Winnipeg's underworld.

"Don't come in here again," the big man told the bloodied one. "If I so much as hear you've been bugging my girl, they'll pull more than a few bits of glass out of your head." He pulled the other man closer. "Know what I mean?"

The man nodded and the big guy headbutted him square in the nose, then let go of the man's hair. The man dropped to his knees, cradling his face. The big guy sauntered off into a corner and swiped another fella's beer from him. The other man backed off and let him have it.

Every nerve inside Gabriel told him to go over to the man on the floor and see if he was all right, but he couldn't. Not like this, in this place. He wasn't even himself here, but instead was dressed in jeans, a brown leather jacket, a wrinkly button-down, messy hair and five o'clock stubble. He even put a touch of purple eye shadow under his eyes to give himself that barely-slept look. In this place—and the others like it that he'd been frequenting the past couple of months—he went by Mike. A common name and one easily forgettable.

The dude with his face all bloodied slowly got to his feet and headed toward the bathroom in the back.

Gabriel returned to the bar where his beer had been knocked over in the tussle. He righted the bottle. It was near empty. He sat down on the stool, massaged the back of his neck, then checked the clock. It was twelve after one in the morning. The place would let out at two.

The barkeep came by. Whether the bartender was Dave himself, Gabriel didn't know, but it was the same barkeep every time he came here.

"Need another?" the man said, voice scratchy, probably from years of smoking given the pack of Players in his breast pocket.

"One more," Gabriel said, "and make it a Keith's this time."

"Sure thing." The man poured the beer from the tap for this one, then passed the pint to Gabriel.

"Five and a quarter."

Gabriel paid up.

The mission in these places was simple: sit there, shut up and listen. Get up once in a while, walk around casually, then go right back to his spot at the bar. If the bar didn't have stools in front of it, get a small table off to the side. Stay incognito and not do anything to draw attention to himself. If someone talked to him, give them the time of day, but don't reveal any personal details or actual events of his life. He was Mike in these places, and Mike was a different man altogether. Gabriel had given him a backstory, one that he'd yet to share. The downside was Mike didn't have an ID and Gabriel didn't want to be caught forging any—and he didn't know how to forge one convincingly—so that was his only link to his real life outside of these bars. Bouncers were pretty strict checking for age, even in a place like Dave's.

Depending where he went, sometimes the Axiom-man uniform stayed home. Some places patted you down before entering and the last thing he wanted was for some bouncer wondering why his clothes felt unusually thick or what that metal thing in his pants was if he patted the Axiom-man belt buckle beneath his shirt. He had the suit on beneath his clothes tonight though.

"Hey kid, we only got a little left to go and then it's time to run. Wanna buy me a drink?" The woman's voice sounded low and throaty.

Gabriel turned to look at her. "Barely got enough for myself. Sorry."

"Yeah right. Could just say, 'No, I don't like you.'"

"It's not like that."

The woman wasn't half-bad. Decent figure, black hair with tight ringlets, eyes accented to look like a cat's. She wasn't his dream girl, but she wasn't appalling either.

Getting involved with women was off the table. Not even the actual getting involved with them, but simply getting tangled up with one even under the character of Mike was out of the question. He didn't want to be responsible for looking out for anyone even if that meant forfeiting the company of a lovely lady for the evening.

The barkeep came by again. "Need anything, Miss?"

She nodded at Gabriel. "Yeah, this fella right here said he'd buy me a round."

"No, I didn't." Gabriel kept his voice firm.

The bartender looked at him as if questioning what to do.

The woman scooted over closer and whispered in his ear: "Come on, hottie, just one. I promise it'll be worth it."

"Not. Happening." Gabriel picked up his drink and left his spot. The woman cursed after him. He didn't care. All eyes were on them for a brief moment before folks went back to their drinks and conversation.

The man who'd been bloodied up came out of the bathroom and was back circulating again. Gabriel even saw him exchange a few words with the guy who'd beaten him up and it didn't come to blows.

Never know in these places, Gabriel thought.

He leaned up against the wall and watched a couple of Joes play pool. Aside from the scuffle earlier, tonight had been pretty non-informative. A couple of mentions of lighting up some dope outside, one guy saying how he bought some beer for a handful of teenagers, and some info on a couple women out back who made a living via the world's oldest profession.

Part of the goal of hanging out here was familiarizing himself with a side of the city he didn't know too well. Gabriel's experience with the inner city was only based on what he saw as Axiom-man. He'd grown up in a comfortable area, was sheltered from the ugly side of life for the most part, the only glimpses of it whatever he happened to catch on the news when flipping through the channels. He went to a nice school, and even when he struck out on his own, he lived in a nice apartment in a relatively safe area downtown. Nothing edgy.

As Axiom-man, he was confined to only one facet of his mission. He patrolled from the sky or from rooftops and swooped in when needed. When a super-powered threat arose, he met it head-on. The petty crime he stopped, too, but he'd come to realize that the petty crimes were symptoms of a much deeper issue. Sure, some of it was people simply being mean to others, but the dealers, the prostitutes, the gangs—there was structure behind them. Whether several structures or one giant one, he wasn't sure, but there had to be a way to put an end to it. The people in this city needed to change to avert the risk of any other major disasters from happening.

The black clouds from the Doorway of Darkness were out there. Perhaps they were affecting people and how they behaved? Or perhaps they needed direct interaction with people to transform them into something more powerful? Either way, cleaner streets meant less of a chance of the wrong kind of person coming into contact with these clouds thus diminishing the chances of creating another villain like Bleaken.

The city was still recovering from the chaos of that day when the whole city was blanketed in a cloud of darkness.

Even Gabriel was still recovering, both as Axiom-man and Gabriel Garrison. He knew that ultimately the black cloud that affected Tom and Payton was his fault by allowing the Doorway of Darkness to open all that time ago. He should have stopped Redsaw sooner. Now those clouds were in the world and changing things, creating monsters, and who knew what else. To make matters worse, they seemed to materialize and disappear without warning, thus making them impossible to track down.

As Gabriel—he was alone. After rescuing Valerie from the men who kidnapped her, he hadn't spoken to her since visiting her in the hospital as Axiom-man and her revealing she knew who he really was. She had called him a monster after he beat to a pulp one of the men that nearly killed her. He didn't know if she was still all shook up over it and was taking it out on him, or if she really meant it. She hadn't called him since that day, and he had respected her wishes to be left alone.

Heartache plagued him daily and, he admitted, being Mike and going to places like these helped mask that hollow pain. He had to be careful and not lose himself in Mike. Mike didn't care about things like women, responsibility or the welfare of others. That was also one of the reasons why he didn't interfere with the fight earlier aside from trying to fly beneath folks' radars.

Gabriel took the final swig of his beer and set the glass down on the nearest table. Hands in his pockets, he did one more lap around the room, ears open, then glanced at the clock. It was ten to two.

Debating whether to call it a night or not, he caught sight of a blonde girl in the corner, leaning up against the wall near the furthest pool table. She hadn't been there a second ago. In the bathroom and just come out, maybe? One of the tricks he'd learned since doing these bar rounds was to keep track of everyone in the room, memorize faces. He figured doing so would help him in the big picture whether seeing them on the street at a later time or even running into them as Axiom-man.

But this girl—she seemed too young to be here. She looked sixteen, maybe seventeen, wore a white T-shirt and blue jeans. Drinking age was eighteen. She simply looked either too young for her real age, or she had a fake ID, or someone snuck her in. Gabriel found an empty table near the pool tables and pretended to occupy himself looking at the coasters and happy hour menu while stealing glances at the girl in the corner.

She was playing pool with a couple of guys who appeared at least ten years her senior. She seemed to have a handle on things, tightly brushing past them when it was her turn, touching them occasionally on the shoulder or chest and giving them a gentle smile. It was a beautiful smile, too.

"Hang on . . ." Gabriel said under his breath. One of the guys picking up a cue was the big dude from earlier, the one who bloodied the other guy's nose, probably even broke it. The big man talked to the girl, suddenly transforming from a behemoth of toughness to an awkward oaf who seemed to stand there shuffling and barely keeping his balance like he had two left feet.

Gabriel scanned the coaster in his hands and the palm tree image. *Puerto Vallarta. If only I had the money to go there. Sure, remind us here in Winnipeg of the tropics when our national tree is a frozen pine.*

A loud bell rang from the bar. "'Kay, folks, that's it!"

The clock on the wall read just past two.

Gabriel fought the urge to stand. That young girl in the corner was probably Katie, the girl that big guy made such a stink about earlier. She was way too young for him, and while people hooked up regardless of age, something didn't sit right, and Gabriel resolved to keep an eye on her.

The bell rang again and the barkeep shouted, "I said get out. Thanks for coming, but get out. We open again at eleven."

People started heading toward the door.

Gabriel remained and watched the girl, who still hung around the pool tables.

CHAPTER TWO

2:42 A.M. - OUTSIDE DAVE'S BAR

IF THAT WAS Dave behind the counter, he might've been the kind of guy who could talk tough but didn't back it up. It took a while to convince everyone the place was closed and for them to get outside.

Gabriel stuck around until Dave gave him a dirty look that said, "Get out or I don't want to see you come in here anymore."

The blonde—Katie, her name might be—and the group she was with were the last to leave.

Outside Dave's Bar, Gabriel hung around at the corner across the street, head dipped low, lighting a cigarette. He hated these things and they tasted terrible. He was careful not to inhale for his own sake and only did so when others were watching. He coughed nearly every time and felt like an idiot , too.

The blonde and the group of guys hung around outside Dave's Bar yapping until the green-glowing neon sign went off and only the couple of streetlights from the alley lit the corner. The regular streetlamps were out on the bar's side of the road. Soon, their group dispersed, with Katie and the big guy walking down the street, his arm around her.

Gabriel kept his distance and watched them as they headed down the street. He debated suiting up and hitting the rooftops, but these nightly missions were for intel and Axiom-man wasn't welcome unless needed. Right now, a girl and her guy weren't exactly a shoe-in for a 911 to the hero in blue.

Once Katie and the big dude were a few blocks away, Gabriel kept to his side of the street and started following them. He wasn't expecting anything to happen, but she was so young-looking that he couldn't help but feel obligated to keep an eye on her to at least ensure she made it home safely.

The streets were pretty quiet for nearly 3 A.M. A few rowdies shouted profanities as they horsed around in parking lots and on sidewalks. A couple tires screeched. A few bottles shattered against the pavement. A siren rose on the air in the distance.

Another night in Winnipeg.

Gabriel walked past another group of people, squeezing in between them when the group of four didn't let him step to the side but instead purposely kept in his way.

"Hey punk, you like shoving past me?" one of the guys said.

Gabriel kept going, and patted his jacket for the Winnipeg Jets baseball cap he kept inside along with a pair of shades. If things got ugly and he had to activate his powers, his hair would take on a blue hue and blue energy would coat his eyes. The hat and glasses would help conceal that and, hopefully, make the change go unnoticed in the heat of the moment.

"Yo, I was talkin' to you, man!" the guy shouted after him.

Just ignore him, Gabriel told himself. Something clunked him in the back of his head and the light metallic *ting* of an aluminum pop can hitting the sidewalk told him what it was. He glanced over his shoulder and the guy who threw it—some punk in a black jacket and green baseball cap with a straight brim turned partly to the side—tossed his hands into the air as if asking, "What're you going to do about it?"

Gabriel just gave his head a slight shake and kept on. "Not worth my time."

"Yeah, you better keep going. You don't want any of this."

"And you don't want to see what I'm capable of," Gabriel said under his breath.

He kept his ears open to make sure the group of guys weren't following him. Though he wasn't afraid of them, he just wasn't in the mood. After spending so much time hanging around people like the ones that just taunted him, he realized that a lot of them were just folks having a bad day. It didn't excuse their behavior, but it gave him the knowledge that what was clearly a display of evil on the surface wasn't always true of what was going on inside of a person. Part of these nightly missions were to understand those he was fighting against not only in terms of their actions, but motivations, thoughts, feelings and more.

Katie and her guy stopped up against a brownstone a couple sidewalk lengths away. They stood at the foot of the steps, the dude's hands resting on her hips, hers resting on his chest. Gabriel felt awkward for staring so he kept his head down and hid his glance. They couldn't tell where he was looking as long as he kept his head facing forward.

When he was about even with them on the other side of the street, he involuntarily slowed his pace. She *seemed* to be home safe and sound. Whether she was going to invite the guy up, he didn't know, but if she was underage, maybe they were outside *his* place? Was the dude forcing her to come up? If she *was* underage, should he step in?

Gabriel got about a sidewalk length ahead then crouched down as if to tie his shoe. The guy gave the girl a shove toward the front door. She stumbled a few steps and Gabriel fought the urge to spring into action. A push wasn't enough to get involved. Then she started giggling and the guy followed her up the steps. Soon the two were inside the brownstone and were gone.

Gabriel went up to the corner, stood there, eyed the brownstone one last time, then kept going.

A few minutes later, a car came peeling down the street, the shriek of its tires enough to cause him to spin around. The car came to a screeching halt outside the brownstone, riding up onto the curb. The door opened and a body tumbled out the back door. The door was quickly closed and the car peeled off down the sidewalk before coming down off the curb and back onto the street.

You're not getting away, Gabriel thought and put on his baseball hat. He *shifted* and activated his powers, filling his eyes with blue energy and delivering a lightning-quick bolt of energy to two of the car's tires, causing it to fall into a free spin and the driver to put on the brakes. The car slammed up against a lamppost, knocking the thing over in a loud crash.

Gabriel *shifted* and turned his powers off. He ran over to the payphone on the corner.

"911. What's your emergency?"

"Yeah, I got a guy on Garry Street that was just dumped from a vehicle. I can see the blood on his face from here. You need to send an ambulance out."

"Make and color of the car?"

"Four-door Explorer. Black. Looks like it crashed further up the street."

"Did you see this happen?"

"Saw it happen. Going to check in on the guy on the ground now."

"We'll send a car and an ambulance. Stay there until the paramedics arrive. What is your name?"

"Just 'Anonymous' is fine."

"And what number are you calling from?"

Gabriel hung up and ran to the guy on the ground. He kept an eye on the black Explorer further up to see if anyone was going to get out of the car. He hoped he hadn't accidentally killed anyone.

The man lying on the ground moaned and Gabriel got in close. The guy's face was covered in blood, both his eyes swollen, and his right cheek was split open.

"It's okay, man," Gabriel said, "help is on the way."

The man just groaned.

"Just talk to me. What's your name?"

The guy went into a coughing fit and leaned over on his side. Blood gushed out of his mouth and splashed onto the pavement.

Might need to fly him to the hospital unless the EMTs get here ASAP, Gabriel thought.

Metal screeching followed by a bang came from the end of the street. Two guys whose faces Gabriel couldn't make out from where he was hobbled out of the car then, catching sight of him, suddenly found the strength to sprint in his direction.

"Oh great," Gabriel said.

The man on the ground craned his neck back, taking a peek. With tears in his voice, he said, "They'll kill me, man. They'll . . . they'll kill us. Get me out of here."

Gabriel pulled his shades out from his jacket and got ready to power up. The brownstone's door flew open and the big guy and Katie came running down the stone steps and stopped at the body.

"Tee-lo?" the big guy said.

Katie gave Gabriel a cold stare.

The big guy stormed over to Gabriel, grabbed him, pulled him off the ground and held him up, his feet dangling a few inches from the sidewalk. "You're a dead man." He cocked his fist and just before he let it fly into Gabriel's face, Katie said, "Ben," and pointed in the direction of the two guys running toward them, guns drawn.

They stormed over, meaning business, the gun barrels alternating between pointing at Gabriel, Ben, Katie and the guy on the ground.

"Better put those away as the cops are already en route," Gabriel said, keeping his voice firm. He almost used his Axiom-man voice, but caught himself. Not that these guys had probably ever heard it, but should he ever run into them in the future as Axiom-man, he didn't want them stringing two and two together. If they even remembered his voice at that point. Better safe than sorry.

"Ben, drop him," Katie said.

The big guy looked at her as if she was crazy. "This guy took out Tee-lo, do you really think—"

"No, you idiot," she said. "*Those* guys took out Tee-lo. This guy's done nothing."

Ben gave Gabriel a violent shake as if to cement himself as the alpha male before dropping Gabriel to his feet.

Sirens rose on the air and panic immediately filled the eyes of the men with the guns. They reaffirmed their aim.

"Pick 'im up. Now," one of them said.

Stall him, Gabriel said. *The cops'll get here and—* Katie was crouched down beside Tee-lo, already scooping her arms under his body. She was small, but she seemed to have a fit physique, like the body of a gymnast or dancer. Still, Gabriel didn't want her to pick up Tee-lo on her own and it sure didn't look like Ben was going to be of any help.

He crouched down beside Tee-lo and got his hands under his body.

Katie adjusted herself and her arms, bringing her head nearly right up to Gabriel's. At first he thought she was going to help him lift Tee-lo, but then realized she was coming in close for a reason.

Quietly, she said, "Just do as they say or you're going to get everyone killed."

The sirens grew louder.

Gabriel nodded and Katie pulled back. With Tee-lo under his arms, Gabriel staggered to his feet, wishing he could activate his powers thus his ultra strength to make the job easier.

"Bring him in," Ben said, nodding toward the brownstone's door.

One of the guys with a gun led the way with Katie by his side, Gabriel holding Tee-lo next, then Ben, then the other armed man bringing up the rear.

The sirens grew closer.

This has got to be temporary, Gabriel thought. *They'll see the blood outside, the crashed car, and they'll know we're in here.*

They entered the brownstone and the door closed behind them.

CHAPTER THREE

3:13 A.M. - THE BROWNSTONE

TEE-LO LAY ON the carpet of the corner suite on the third floor. Blood leaked from the corners of his lips and ran down his chin. Gabriel, Ben and Katie stood across from him, hands on their heads as instructed, the two men with the guns standing on the other side of Tee-lo's body, firearms aimed at them.

"All right, who called the cops?" the first guy with the gun said. "He'll be the first to die." Gabriel's heart leapt into his throat. "And take your stupid sunglasses off," the gunman added, before coming over to Gabriel and swatting them off his face. "It's the middle of the night."

Gabriel didn't flinch. *Mike* didn't flinch. *Might as well keep up appearances.*

Back on the other side of the body, the gunman asked again: "Who called the cops?"

The sirens were loud and right outside. They remained on for a few more seconds before shutting off.

They're out front, Gabriel thought. *Good. They'll be in here soon enough.* He just hoped that "soon enough" was soon-soon, but by the time the cops banged on every door in the brownstone, it might already be too late.

The man kicked Tee-lo in the ribs. Tee-lo yelped. "I'll ask again: who called the cops!"

Gabriel swallowed, about to speak up, when Katie said, "I did."

"No, you didn't," Ben said. "I was with you the whole time."

"Not when I went into the washroom you weren't," she said.

"You don't even have a cell phone."

The gunman kicked Tee-lo again. "All right, shut up!" Clearing his throat, he added, "Then I know who's going to die first."

Gabriel glanced at Katie. She was already looking at him. She knew he had been the one to call the cops. Her gaze also said he shouldn't try and stand up for her to set the record straight.

"You can kill me if you want," she said, "but I think you should kill Tee-lo first. After all, looks like you guys failed the first time."

The second gunman spoke. "We didn't fail. We dropped him off to send you a message."

"Shut up!" the first gunman said. "Don't tell them our plan."

If things don't get better real quick then I'm going to have no choice but to power up and take those guys out, Gabriel thought.

"Check the window," the first gunman told the other. The second complied and quickly went to the window that overlooked the front of the building. He peeked between a crack in the curtains. "There's two cars, three officers. A fourth is still in his vehicle. An ambulance is down by our car. One of the officers is looking at the blood on the ground." The second gunman quickly backed away from the window, nearly tripping over his own feet as he did so.

"What?" the first gunman asked.

"He looked up. I don't know if he saw me."

The gunman's breathing immediately picked up pace as panic began to settle in. He eyed the group. "We kill them then take the fire escape. It's close enough to the parkade beside this place. We hop over and get out."

The second gunman nodded.

Katie lowered her hands and crossed her arms. "Still think you should kill Tee-lo first." She glanced down at him. "I mean, look at him. He's half dead as it is. Just pop one between his eyes and—"

"Shut up!" Ben shouted and slapped her.

"Hey!" The first gunman had the barrel aimed squarely at Ben.

Ben put his hands back up.

"You hit like a girl," Katie said. Her cheek was already deep red from the strike. She stole a glance at Gabriel and gave him a quick wink.

He furrowed his brow.

"Hands up," the gunman told Katie.

"Not until you shoot Tee-lo first," she said and crossed her arms even tighter to her body.

What is she doing? Gabriel wondered. *She's going to get us all killed.* He might be a superhero, but he wasn't bulletproof even with his powers activated. He was going to give it another moment or two and then power up and put an end to this before it got worse.

The second gun man was beside his comrade, the two squarely aiming their pistols on the others.

"I think you deserve to die first," the gunman told Katie.

"If that's what you think is best, but you should remove the obstacle between us and make it easier on yourself."

"What do you mean obstacle? I have a gun."

The other gunman said, "Don't argue with her. Just shoot her."

"Come on, Mr. Big Shot," Katie said. "Shoot the guy on the floor. Grant me my last request, then you can kill me."

"Oh, I'm going to kill you." He aimed at Katie.

"But shoot the guy on the floor."

"Don't listen to her," his friend said, "it's a trick."

"Don't kill me," Tee-lo groaned.

"It's no trick," she said.

"What are you doing?" Ben asked.

"Just shoot the guy on the floor and I'll raise my hands and you can shoot me anywhere you want."

"I'm going to get you between the eyes."

"As if you're that good a shot," she said.

What's going on? Gabriel thought.

"Kill the guy on the floor and you can take a step closer," she said.

"No, not m-me!" Tee-lo shouted, then coughed up another wave of blood.

"Yes, you. You have to go first."

"No, not me. Not ever!" Tee-lo rolled to his feet and started toward the door. He could barely walk, but Gabriel had to hand it to the guy for trying.

Both gunmen aimed their guns at Tee-lo and in an instant Katie was on them. The guns went off and Tee-lo hit the floor. Katie had one of the gunman's wrists in her hand and jerked his bodyweight toward the ground. The moment he pitched forward, she struck him in the nose with her palm, snapping his head back. Quickly, she struck him in the ear, throwing off his balance and dragging him down even further so she was able to step over his arm so his elbow was between her legs. She pulled up and broke it. The other gunman had his weapon aimed at her. Gabriel tackled him. The gun went off and Gabriel didn't know if someone got hit, but he thought he heard Ben go down. After breaking the first gunman's arm, Katie kicked him in the head with the ball of her foot, first in the forehead then, when he pitched forward from the daze, hit him on the ledge of the skull with her heel, putting him out for good. Gabriel and the other gunman wrestled on the floor and Katie quickly intervened and dropped her knee down on the other gunman's throat then gave a quick strike to the man's temple. He, too, was out.

Ben was on all fours beside them, wheezing and catching his breath.

"Oh come on, you big baby," Katie said, helping him to his feet.

For such a big guy, he didn't seem all that tough anymore. He appeared free of injury.

"How'd you do that?" Ben asked her, clearly taken off guard by her display of martial skill.

The rush of footsteps echoing down the hallway signaled the cops' arrival.

Gabriel didn't want to be arrested and, he knew, neither did Katie and Ben.

"What about Tee-lo?" Gabriel asked so Katie wouldn't have to give an explanation on how she knew how to fight like that.

Tee-lo groaned. "Don't mind me. I'll be fine."

Gabriel saw the blood by Tee-lo's legs and assumed he got tagged somewhere below the waist.

"He'll be all right," Katie said. "Let's go."

"We're not taking this guy," Ben said, thumbing in Gabriel's direction.

Katie looked at Gabriel. "You're right. He does look kind of weak, like he won't be able to pull his own out there. But he did take that other guy to the floor."

"I don't trust him," Ben said.

The rush of footsteps stopped.

Katie's voice became a whisper. "You're right. We shouldn't trust him. He's not one of us."

"Us?" Gabriel said.

Tee-lo moaned. "Anyone have an Aspirin?"

Ben went over to the gun on the floor, picked it up, then came back over to Katie. He pointed the gun at Gabriel. "You, come here."

Not wanting to give himself away, Gabriel complied. He'd find a different way to escape then come back later as Axiom-man and put these two away. When he was close to them, he kept his hands above his head and the three shuffled as one close to the window opposite the door. Keeping the gun on him, Ben opened it. "Those guys knew about the fire escape, which means they scouted us out before all this."

"Can I go first?" Katie asked.

"Sure, babe."

She moved past him. Ben still had the gun trained on Gabriel.

"We should leave him," he said, "and let him explain to the cops what went down."

"Agreed," she said. "Give me the gun."

"What?"

In a blink, she reached around him from behind and grabbed the gun from his hand. The moment he struggled to maintain control of the weapon, the door burst open with two officers coming in. "Put the weapon down! Hands in the air now!"

CHAPTER FOUR

3:31 A.M. - THE BROWNSTONE

"GET ON YOUR knees!" the cop shouted.

Gabriel immediately complied. The only light coming into the room was the moonlight through the window. Though dark, in his peripheral he saw Katie hesitate as she dropped the gun to the ground. She looked his way and it was his turn to give her a wink. She made a face, but then went along with it though he could tell she was hesitating.

Who is this girl? he thought. *She's obviously not who she's pretending to be.*

"Lie down. Now!" the cop shouted, gun still trained on them.

Hands still behind his head, Gabriel adjusted himself so his gaze was on the floor. There was no way he could allow himself to be arrested. If they searched him, they'd find his uniform beneath his clothes. And Katie . . . whoever she was, something told him she wasn't a common criminal, that she was someone special to be able to do what she did. He had to get them both out of here and then figure out their next move and Ben would only slow them down.

The two cops came closer through the dark room.

Gabriel bowed his head to the floor. Thank goodness his baseball hat was still on as it would make what he was about to do even easier, and thanks to the bad lighting, what hair of his that was showing sticking out from the hat would be difficult to see.

Face to the floor, Gabriel *shifted* and activated his powers. Keeping his eyes shut, he let them fill with blue light. He listened carefully for the cops' footfalls to get closer. He knew their eyes were still adjusting to the dark and a sudden shift in lighting would—

He let forth a burst of light from his eyes, igniting the room in bright blue. It was just a burst of light, not a blast, so nothing and no one was harmed, but it was enough to leave the two cops stunned as they went temporarily blind.

Taking advantage of the opportunity, he kicked Ben in the cops' direction, where he crashed into one of them. The two went down, the cop holding onto Ben in a bear hug.

Gabriel grabbed Katie and yanked her toward the window and pulled her out onto the fire escape. He did his best to avert his gaze from her so she couldn't catch sight of his glowing eyes as he pulled her up the fire escape steps. From below, the cops shouted at each other inside the apartment. He quickened his pace. Katie kept up without issue.

"How'd you do that?" she asked.

"Had a flashlight in my pocket," he said.

"Must've been some flashlight."

"One of those tactical ones."

"I see."

Once the two got to the rooftop, they sprinted across.

Still keeping his head turned away from her, Gabriel said, "Those two guys with the guns were going to jump to the parkade. We're going to do the same."

"You realize that's at least a twelve-foot leap, don't you? Those guys didn't think it through. Besides, that's twelve feet just to get across never mind the height differential. The top level of the parkade is higher than this building. You'll have to jump in between the levels just right to make—"

"We'll be fine," he said.

"I don't think you can manage."

Gabriel kept running toward the roof's edge. Katie was right. It wasn't a straight jump across. They'd have to jump in between the levels to get off the roof and angle their bodies so as to not hit anything.

From behind them: "Freeze!"

Not wanting to chance anything, Gabriel slowed a half-step so he could get behind Katie. He grabbed her firmly by the shoulders just as the two approached the edge. Kicking off the ground, he floated them off the edge and, turning their bodies partly to the side, got in between the parkade levels. He did it fast enough and awkwardly enough to make it come across as a lucky leap. He even pulled her down to the ground and rolled with her a few feet just to sell it.

He *shifted* his powers off before looking at her. "Are you okay?"

"Fine," she said.

"Stop right now!" the cop shouted and fired off a shot.

Gabriel and Katie got to their feet and ran to the far side of the parkade and hit the stairwell.

"They're going to radio the guys on the street. We won't make it," she said.

"You're right."

"You need to think things through even under the heat of the moment." Her expression was like venom. "I knew it was you who called the cops and I saw you following me since Dave's. I was trying to do you a favor and you went and messed everything up."

"Me? Who's the one who kung-fued everybody?"

"I saved your life."

"And I saved yours, too."

"Well, you better have a plan to save it again because you and I are both going to jail unless we find a way off this parkade without getting arrested."

At the second level, they went out the door and onto the parkade proper.

"The street's that way," Gabriel said, nodding ahead. "Odds are that's where the squad cars are, if more have come. I didn't hear any sirens but they could've snuck up. Regardless, there's still the two at the corner."

"At least you're keeping track."

Was that playfulness in her voice? Now was not the time! "Can't go up. Can't go down."

"Good, talk it through."

Was she trying to teach him something?

Gabriel glanced to the back of the parkade. The parkade was up against another building and a narrow alley. It was their only exit.

"How are you at parkour?" she asked.

"Not very good," he said, which was true. He was more of a walk or fly kind of guy.

"Mind your grip. Try and relax. When you hit the ground, let yourself collapse in on yourself to help absorb the impact."

She ran over the ledge that overlooked the drop. There was a mere four feet between the parkade and the building wall across from it. It would be a dangerous fall never mind if a person fell and their bodyweight carried them backward so they'd ricochet off the wall before hitting the ground. No telling what they'd break.

Katie climbed up onto the ledge just as they heard scampering footfalls. "Are you coming?"

"Right behind you," he replied.

She disappeared over the edge with the fluidity and grace of a cat. Gabriel *shifted* on his powers and hopped over the edge, using his flight to help him "jump" down to the first level of the parkade and then to the ground. He *shifted* them off just before he hit the pavement.

Katie was already gone. He saw the narrow mouth of the alley off to the side and ran for it. When he emerged out onto the street, he checked for cop cars and, not seeing any, jogged across the street and went in between the buildings on the other side. The next step would be to find a place to change and get off the ground. He could scan for Katie from the air, but he had a feeling she would be hard to find. She seemed like the kind of girl who would only surface if she wanted to be found.

Chapter Five

4:03 A.M. - Outside Dave's Bar

KATIE WAS ALREADY waiting for him by the time Gabriel emerged from the alley across the street from Dave's Bar. He had gone there on foot, ducking in and out of alleyways in an effort to practice keeping out of sight instead of flying as originally planned. A couple of times he had to hide behind a dumpster when he saw a cop car and assumed those in it were looking for someone who matched his description.

"How'd you know I'd be here?" Gabriel asked Katie once coming up to her.

"Rookie mistake, going back to the scene of the crime. In this case, where you first saw me. I knew you wouldn't go home. No one who acts that calm under duress from the cops does. They stay out, believing themselves to be above the law in some way."

She had a point, but he hoped it wasn't true of himself, because as Axiom-man, he did his best to confine himself to the same laws as every other citizen, despite the occasional temptation to feel like he was exempt from them because of what he could do.

"I could say the same thing about you," he said.

"I wouldn't have come here if it wasn't for you. I'm not that stupid."

"And if someone saw you?"

"Then I'd have to be sure they *un*saw me."

"Don't know if I want to know how you'd accomplish that."

"Be better off if you didn't."

Out here, away from the confusion and the large boyfriend, Gabriel finally got a good look at her. She was around five-two, maybe one-ten, one-fifteen, with silky light blonde hair and bright blue eyes. Given her display of combat skills, he had been right about her athleticism earlier and she had the body to back it up.

"What happened back there, um, Katie, right?" Gabriel said.

"You don't want to know."

"It's kind of my business now."

"Doesn't have to be." She held his gaze, as if determining if he was going to stick around.

"I guess all I want to know is if you'll be all right. You're only a kid."

She rolled her eyes. "As if. Please. I'm old enough despite how I might look."

"Eighteen at best."

"You're not that old yourself. You shave off that little bit of shadow and you'll drop five years."

"Still old enough to know you're too young to be hanging around with guys like Ben."

"I'm hanging around with guys like Ben for a reason, and now you've gone and messed that up for me."

"You messed it up for yourself. You were going to leave him for the cops. What kind of a girlfriend does that?"

"Is that what you think?"

"About what?"

"That I'm his girlfriend? Gimme a break. The guy's a pig through and through."

"But the way he was holding you . . ."

"There's reasons for everything and, no, I'm not that kind of girl."

He cocked his head to the side. "You seem awfully open talking to someone you just met."

"Trust me, I'm being more closed than you can imagine, but as long as we're playing this game of 'who are you and what do you want,' what should I call you?"

"Name's Mike."

"Yeah. Indeed." She was clearly being sarcastic.

"Think what you want."

"I will."

"Fine."

"Fine."

The two kept quiet and both stiffened up when the sound of sirens rose on the air. They retreated further into the alley beside Dave's Bar to keep out of sight. When the sirens faded, Katie said, "I'm heading out." She turned to walk away, but before Gabriel could say anything, she turned around and said, "As long as you like playing at being 'Mike,' do you want to come with me and help me get Ben? Be a good story for 'Mike' to tell."

"Ben's off to jail, Katie," Gabriel said.

"They've taken him in for processing. Given how backed up the cops are, he's not sitting in a holding cell just yet."

Gabriel jogged up to her and kept his voice down. "Are you saying you want to break someone out of police custody?"

"I'm saying I need Ben to not be in jail." She was serious. If Ben wasn't her lover or even a friend, then why was he so important?

Gabriel shook his head. "I'm not helping you get someone away from the cops. What about Tee-lo?"

Katie's expression went stern. "You're in over your head, Mike. Go home."

She turned and walked away.

"Katie," Gabriel said.

She kept walking.

CHAPTER SIX

4:15 A.M. - THE ROOFTOPS

KATIE WAS GOOD, Axiom-man would give her that.

He had quickly changed in an alleyway and flew up to the rooftops right after she told him to go away. From his high vantage point, he saw her keep completely out of sight from anyone on street level, doing everything from simply hiding around corners to ducking behind cars, tucking her body tight against the wheel, to sidling up against lampposts and turning around them as people walked past so she was completely hidden from their view. It was as if the city was a giant playground to her and she didn't fear looking out of place if spotted. The way she moved—the grace, the flexibility, the patience and swift movement—it was clear she was not self-taught. Katie had made it all the way from Dave's Bar to the police station on Main keeping completely out of sight.

Axiom-man remained on the roof across the street, perched on the ledge. A couple of cops lingered out front of the station. He considered flying down and warning them about what was going to happen, but at the same time, a part of him was curious to know what Katie was going to do to get Ben out of there.

He checked below to a parked truck where he last saw Katie crouched down behind the rear bumper. She was gone.

"Where the—" He scanned the area and didn't see her.

No one was around the building, just those two cops out front.

Axiom-man waited, keeping an eye out.

As the minutes passed, he more and more convinced himself he should fly down and say something. About to leap off the building ledge, a third cop came around the building, gave the other two a nod, then went in.

She looked familiar.

Katie!

Axiom-man flew off the ledge and headed for the entrance, startling the two cops standing there when he landed.

"You guys are about to have an emergency," he said.

No sooner had he spoken the words, shots were fired inside the station. Axiom-man ran past them and burst in through the doors. The air was filled with smoke and it was difficult to see. Something bigger just happened than a couple guns going off.

"Shut this place down!" someone shouted.

"Get down to the main level. We got—" The person was cut off.

Axiom-man scanned the smoke and could barely make out anything. The two cops from outside caught up with him.

"What in the—"

They drew their weapons.

"Stand guard," Axiom-man said. "Don't let anyone out. And be ready."

The people moving around were all faint shadows against a backdrop of light gray. He tried lighting up his eyes to see if it would make a difference and help him see, but it only made it worse. He quickly turned off his eye beams.

If memory served him, processing was up past the counter and tucked in behind the side door. He headed there, telling every officer he passed he was searching for the assailant and gave them a description, warning she was dressed as one of them. He withheld her name, though.

"Do you know how many blonde cops are on shift tonight?" one of the male officers said. "There's at least six of them."

"One of them is lying unconscious somewhere without her uniform," Axiom-man said. "I suggest checking the cars out back to see what you'd find."

More shots went off behind the side door. Axiom-man ran over to it, opened it and kept to the side of the frame before going in just in case anyone fired at the intrusion.

This room was equally filled with smoke. Either Katie had smoke bombs this whole time, or had set something off in here, perhaps shot at a fire extinguisher and caused it to explode. He didn't see any flames, though.

A handful of cops lay unconscious on the ground, a few others darting around like shadows behind the veil of smoke.

A couple more shots went off, then the crash of glass. Suddenly a loud whoosh arose along with a series of loud, thunking bangs. The air went damp and cool. Someone yelped then made a choking sound as if they'd just gagged on their own tongue. The whoosh sounded like a waterfall. Axiom-man searched for its source and was struck in the leg by something hard, the blow strong enough to take his leg out from under him. When he hit the ground, he saw the metallic object coming for him just in time to bring his hands up over his face and take the blow against his forearms, sending a spike of pain straight through the muscles and deep into the bones. He was suddenly soaked and a blast of water sent him spinning across the floor to the other side of the room.

Smart, he thought. *Fire hose.* The thing wildly flipped and flopped, its heavy metal end banging into desks and smashing drywall as the untamed water had its way. Axiom-man neared the hose; it whipped over in his direction. He dove over it and followed the hopping hose to its source and turned it off.

He scanned the water-logged and smoke-filled room. Cops coughed, and squeaks filled the air as heavy rubber soles walked across wet floor.

"What happened in here?" a male officer said, running into the room. Uncertainty filled his eyes and the disbelief on the guy's face said it all: rookie.

Axiom-man came over to him. "You had a break-in. I followed—" He was cut off when a series of gunshots went off back in the main foyer. He darted in its direction. The cops he left there lay on the floor with two more running out the front door, seemingly in pursuit of somebody.

Axiom-man ran for the door and overheard one of the officers, who had his pistol drawn, say, "Shoot to kill. Don't let her get away with that guy."

Axiom-man stopped short and saw Katie, still in the police uniform, running with a handcuffed Ben into an alleyway across the street. Sirens rose on the air and a few more cops joined the others in pursuit.

"She's dead," Axiom-man said under his breath. He floated into the sky and went after her.

———

4:32 A.M. - THE ALLEY

Katie and Ben came running down the alley before him, three cops on their tail, a few others lagging far behind and just turning the corner. Katie unlocked Ben's cuffs and put them in her uniform's pocket.

Axiom-man hid behind a dumpster and watched the action as Katie and Ben ran past him, the other cops hot on the trail, guns drawn. He noted Katie was unarmed and had only taken the officer's uniform, not weapons.

"Stop right now! Last warning!" the cop shouted. Axiom-man could tell by his tone that any second now he'd pull the trigger.

Can't let them kill her. There's more to this than meets the eye.

The moment the cops came near the dumpster, Axiom-man kicked it into their path, knocking them down and sending them to the ground. He immediately flew up and out of sight in case Katie looked back.

The other cops rounded the dumpster in the middle of the alley while one of them remained behind to check on his fallen comrades.

Axiom-man kept to the rooftops and followed along. The other cops had their guns drawn and had Katie not just turned another corner, they surely would've fired. Axiom-man dove off the roof and swooped down behind the officers and socked them a good one in the back of their heads, knocking them out and letting them tumble to the ground.

"Sorry, guys," he said. "Nothing personal."

He flew back up and over the roof to see Katie and Ben running below. Ben looked winded as all get out. Katie had perfect running form and seemed as though she could go for hours.

Sirens got closer and Axiom-man knew he had to get her out of there otherwise both her and Ben were headed back to the police station. He couldn't openly assist them, though.

There was only one option to get them out and away from here safe and sound so he could find out what was really going on.

4:52 A.M. - BY THE RIVER

Katie lay on the ground and groaned. When she looked up at him, she furrowed her brow and said, "Mike?"

"Saw you running. You fell down." *Thanks to me knocking you and Ben out and flying you away from there.* "The cops were not far away. What's going on?"

She looked over at Ben, who was still unconscious. "Where are we?"

"Under a bridge along the Red." Gabriel adjusted his jacket.

"That's what that smell is." The Red River was never known as a body of clean water.

"Care to tell me what was going on?"

"Care to tell me how you got us here? You didn't carry us both, Mike. That would've been, what? Ten blocks? Twelve?"

"Seems we both have secrets."

"You followed me, huh?"

"Had to. Wanted to make sure you got home safe."

"Yeah, well, that wasn't exactly the plan."

"Care to tell me about it?"

She sat up and rubbed the back of her head. "Feel like I've been hit by a truck."

It wasn't far from the truth. He had clocked her and Ben pretty good. Wanted to make sure they went under so he could fly them to safety. Once he found out what was going on, he'd take her back to the police. Ben, too.

She looked down at her clothes. "Let me ditch this thing." She stood, stripped the uniform off, revealing the white T-shirt and blue jeans she wore earlier. She went to the river bank and threw the uniform in. Gabriel thought it would've been better to keep it as evidence, but there was no real way to say that or even recover it at the moment.

Katie returned and eyed him quizzically as if trying to piece together the last twenty minutes. Gabriel didn't want her thinking about it too hard so he said, "We should wake him up."

She gave Ben a hit on the chest. "Ben, wake up." He didn't move. She leaned over him and slapped his cheek. "Wake up, Ben."

He groaned and put the palm of his hand to his forehead. "So hung over." He blinked his eyes open, then sat up abruptly. He was clearly dizzy. "What—what's going on?" Looking at Gabriel, he said, "What're you doing here?"

"He saved our lives," Katie said.

Ben chuckled. "Yeah, right." He glanced around, then looked at Katie. "Wait, where's your uniform?"

"Just got rid of it. Besides, it's not *my* uniform."

"Looked hot."

She gave him a sweet smile.

He grinned like a goof, then said, "Where are the cops? Where are we?"

"Out of the way," Gabriel said. *Keep it together. Play it tough. Something's going down and these two are big time involved. Nobody tries to break someone out of police custody unless it's important.*

"Yeah, well, thanks. Whatever you did," Ben said. "Now get out of here."

"You crazy?" Gabriel said. "Cops got a glimpse of me, man. I go out there alone and I'm dead." It wasn't true, but they didn't know that.

"He could rat us out," Katie said.

"He does and he's a dead man," Ben snapped.

"I'll be in jail," Gabriel said. "You won't be able to kill me in there."

"Jail for what?"

"For resisting arrest, maybe dropping a police officer or two. Do you really want to know?" He was kind of enjoying this.

Katie smirked. "We need to lay low for a while, stay out of sight."

Ben ran his fingers through his hair. "Tee-lo's probably ratted us out by now and the fuzz is probably combing the old place."

Gabriel wanted to ask for what, but he didn't. Best to keep quiet and just learn what he could.

"S'okay, I got back up. Always prepared," Ben said. He took Katie by the hand and got to his feet first, then pulled her up. He swayed on his heels. Katie didn't.

Gabriel stood as well.

"Where to?" she asked Ben.

Ben kept his eyes on Gabriel the whole time. "I got a place, don't worry about that. It's a little far from here. Might need to cab it."

"We should walk," Katie said.

"Too far."

"You said a little far." She looked to Gabriel.

"I'm good with either," he said.

"Let's stick to the side of the road," Ben said, "and flag down a cab if we see one."

CHAPTER SEVEN

5:24 A.M. - THE BUNGALOW

THEY DIDN'T FIND a cab, which, Gabriel supposed, was probably for the best. He doubted the cops notified any cabbies about suspects in the area, but better safe than sorry. They made it to a small brick-covered bungalow on foot. When they got in the door, Gabriel guessed the whole house was no more than eight hundred square feet. Judging by the sparse furniture and the only wall decoration being a small hallway mirror, he figured this was a place meant to just lay low and stay out of society's way for a while.

Ben flicked on the light, nodded to the two black pleather sofas in the front room, and said, "Make yourselves at home." He went down the hallway to the kitchen beyond.

Gabriel and Katie entered the living room. He heard a door open then close. Katie peered into the hallway then disappeared around the corner for a moment before coming back.

"He's in the bedroom," she whispered. "Heard him talking to someone."

"Should go listen and hear what he's saying."

"I already know," she said and hugged her elbows.

Gabriel waited a moment and when Katie didn't continue, he asked her what she meant.

"He's checking in with some people about Tee-lo, see what Tee-lo said. The guy's a squealer."

"Who's he talking to?"

"Tee-lo? He'd be squawking to the cops right now."

"I meant Ben." He furrowed his brow. "You mean Ben's in with the cops? Is that how he's finding out about Tee-lo?"

Katie quickly came up to him. "Keep your voice down and listen to me carefully."

He leaned in close to show her he was listening, so much so his cheek brushed up against hers.

"You were in the wrong place at the wrong time, Mike, and you made it worse by following me to the police station. How you got out us out of that mess—Listen, I'm only telling you this because I can relate" —he pulled back an inch— "about being at the wrong place at the wrong time," she said. "If you want to get out of tonight alive, you're going to have to do what I say, when I say it."

"What do you mean, 'alive'?" He thought perhaps he should leave, change into his gear and then monitor things from a bird's eye view. "Maybe I should take off. You could tell Ben something came up."

"You head out that door, you won't make it home. When he's done yapping to the cops, he'll call some people. More than likely, they're already on their way over and they already got your description. You're a part of this, and I need you to just trust me on this, okay? I don't want you to get hurt."

"You make it sound like something big is going down."

"Because something is. Tee-lo was dropped off in front of Ben's other place all beat up as a message not to mess with who Ben was dealing with." She shook her head. "Why did you have to get involved, Mike?"

A part of him wished he could tell her—not that he was Axiom-man, but someone who cared about others and didn't want to see them get hurt. But "Mike" wasn't like that, though he suspected Katie saw right through his persona and wasn't letting on she knew he wasn't who he claimed to be. "Who is Ben, anyway? He's got a place in the city, a place here."

She didn't answer.

After an awkward silence, he asked, "So . . . what's our next move?"

The door down the hallway opened and Katie immediately did a quick shuffle back, giving some distance between them. Ben came into the room, cell phone in hand.

"Tee-lo's dead," Ben said.

"What?" Katie said. "I thought the cops got him."

"They did, but someone busted in on the ambulance when they were trying to get around another car at a red light. Took out the paramedics and dragged Tee-lo from the vehicle. The cops following got hit, too. Word is someone took a baseball bat to Tee-lo's head once they got him to talk."

Gabriel pressed his tongue to the roof of his mouth to keep from asking what Tee-lo knew that was so important that someone would kill him for it. His heart ached. Tee-lo had been in that ratty apartment earlier and had he reacted differently, even made a more obvious display of superpowers, he could've gotten them all out and simply interrogated them as Axiom-man then left them for the cops while he followed up—with or without the police—on whatever they told him.

It's my fault, he thought.

"Are we just going to stay here?" Katie asked.

"Got some people coming over. Big people." He checked the screen on his phone. "Protection," he said quietly.

"I'm scared," Katie said.

Gabriel didn't believe her.

Ben touched her cheek. "Don't worry, baby. Got some guys coming by and they'll help lock this place down." His phone rang and he answered it. "Yep." He looked at Gabriel then down to the floor. "I know." Ben turned around and left the room again, going into the bedroom like before.

Katie was already by Gabriel's side. She said, "Tee-lo would've spilled the beans on everything. Whoever got him is looking for Ben and, most likely, know about this place. Whatever muscle Ben's got on their way better get here quick."

Things were getting too weird and too vague and Gabriel'd had enough. Sounded like a gang war was going on—or about to start—and he couldn't let it escalate any further. He considered finding a moment to himself and getting in touch with the cops and letting them sort it out, but he knew Katie wouldn't let him out of her sight. He had no choice but to trust this girl he'd just met who was clearly not who she seemed.

Just then the bedroom banged open and Ben came storming in with a gun pointed directly at Gabriel.

Chapter Eight

"BEN, ARE YOU crazy, what are you doing!" Katie screamed.

The man stood only four feet away from Gabriel, gun aimed point blank at his chest.

"Search him, Katie," Ben said.

"What?"

"I said search him!"

She hesitated then came over and patted Gabriel down, his legs, arms, jacket. When she patted his waist, she paused when her hands came across his middle and searched his waistline for concealed weapons. Her hand lingered a moment on his Axiom-man belt buckle, which was tucked in behind the button of his jeans. Katie's eyes did a dance and his heart skipped a beat. He wasn't sure if she knew what it was or not.

She pulled her hands away and said, "He's clean."

Ben kept the gun on him. "Good. Get back here."

She obeyed.

To Gabriel, he sternly said, "Have a seat." His cold eyes followed Gabriel as he found a seat on the nearest sofa.

Ben adjusted himself so he remained in front of Gabriel the whole time, gun poised. "What's your name, punk?"

Gabriel steeled himself. He wasn't afraid of Ben, but was concerned how he'd react if things got out of control and the gun went off. He didn't want Katie to get caught in the crossfire. "Mike."

"Mike," Ben said, nodding. "You a cop?"

Gabriel guffawed. "You kidding? Not with my record."

"Your 'record,' huh?" He obviously wasn't buying it.

Convince him. "Yeah, my 'record.'" He mimicked the mockery to help level the field. "I'm not hardcore, I'll tell you that, but I've put my fists in a fair share of people's faces, destruction of property, been in some bad places with a lot of blood and a lot of death." He said it straight-laced, no flinching, all authentic.

Because it was all true.

Ben eyed him intently, weighing his words. "How you know Tee-lo?"

"He was bleeding out in front of your apartment. Wanted to see what was up. Thought I could rob him." He raised his hands palms out to gain Ben's trust. "That's being honest." *I hate lying.* "Guy had nothing worth taking."

Ben quickly raised his eyebrows and nodded slightly as if agreeing with him.

He's coming around. "So whatever. I got caught up in your little evening and now here we are."

"How'd you get us away from the cops?"

Katie held his gaze. He searched her eyes thinking maybe there was something specific she wanted him to say. Her stare was like steel, her blue eyes now cool, and he wasn't sure if that little moment of kindness she showed him earlier had been a ruse or not.

What can I possibly say that he'll believe?

"Let's get talking, Mike, or I'm going to give your face another opening to speak from."

Katie put her hand on Ben's shoulder. "He probably doesn't know. You know how it is, how things get confusing when running from the cops, the fear of arrest, the—"

"I ain't afraid of getting arrested, you know that," he snapped at her. "Was already taken in tonight as it is. If I go in again, I go in again. I don't stay in there long."

"What I meant was things happen so fast in the heat of the moment that all of us have a gap in our memory. Isn't that right, Mike?" She looked at him as if wanting him to agree with her.

"Yeah, that's right," Gabriel said.

"Don't start," Ben said. "I'm not stupid." To Katie, "And you, why you suddenly on his side?"

"I'm not on his side. I'm on yours. Always have been. Just saying that's probably what happened and you pointing a gun at him is only making him panic. You really think you're going to get a straight answer waving a gun in his face?"

"I always get a straight answer from anybody this way." He took a step closer to Gabriel and realigned the barrel of the gun so it was in line with Gabriel's nose. "What's it going to be, Mikey?"

"Don't. Call. Me. Mikey."

"Shut up. I can call you whatever I want. I'm the one with the gun. You going to talk or do you want to join Tee-lo on the other side?"

"Your guys are going to be here soon," Katie said. "Just leave it."

"Man, shut up," Ben said and shoved her to the ground.

She hit the hardwood floor with a thud.

The gun in his face quickly pulled Gabriel's attention away from her.

"I think we have a cop here, Katie. I don't care what he says. Probably knocked us out, took the heat off, set us up. Can't have that."

"Think I'm a cop?" Gabriel said. "Told you that's impossible."

"Yeah, because you're such a bad guy with a big rap sheet, yada, yada, yada." He pressed the barrel of the gun to Gabriel's forehead.

"Fine, you want the truth? I'll tell you: you fainted, Ben, pure and simple."

Ben's face twisted. "As if. My head was pounding after. Besides, how could two people faint? Gimme a break. I'm counting to three then I'm going to make you 'faint,' got it? One, two, thr—"

"He's telling the truth," Katie said.

"What?"

"We were running and you passed out."

"Oh come on!"

"I'm serious!"

What's she doing?

"Panic induces fear and anxiety. You were hopped up on booze and those other pills you took earlier. Throw in a run-in with the cops plus all the excitement of me busting you out of the precinct and the sudden exertion of running—sorry, Ben, you clocked out."

"But my head? I got a welt at the back of my skull."

"You got a welt on the back of your skull because you dropped to your knees and fell straight backward and smacked your head. Mike was running behind us, caught up, and told me where the cops were. Him and I picked you up and ran like crazy and got away." She rounded in front of him and pushed the gun out of the way. "That's the truth."

Ben grimaced as he processed the story. "But you were out, too."

"I wasn't. Sorry. Didn't want to make you feel bad."

Gabriel braced himself for Ben to shove her away and open fire. If it came to that, he'd have no choice but to power up and get himself and Katie to safety.

If he didn't die first.

Ben pulled the gun back, his eyes on Gabriel the whole time. "Fine. Whatever," he muttered. "I'm going to be watching him, though."

Katie rounded back to Ben's side. "Me, too."

Chapter Nine

6:01 A.M. - THE BUNGALOW

"CARS ARE PULLING up," Katie said, then stepped back from peeking out from the front room's curtains.

"A couple'll stay in the cars, watch the house. A couple other guys are coming in," Ben said.

Gabriel still sat on the sofa, instructed to just stay put. All he could do right now was simply sit, wait and listen. He was also worried about his day job at the call centre. He'd been on shaky ground for a long time because his Axiom-man activities had wreaked havoc on his attendance. If he missed work today or even part of his shift, he was pretty sure he'd be shown the door if he didn't come home to a nasty voicemail from his boss telling him he was through first. He needed that job, too, and he didn't have enough of a savings cushion to get him past a single month's rent.

A minute later, there was a knock on the door. Ben went up to it and peeked through the keyhole.

He cursed and ducked.

A second later shots rang out and blasted the handle from the door. A big guy with dark skin and a black suit kicked it open and stormed in. He rounded the door and picked up Ben from the other side by the collar. Two other guys came in, guns aimed, both equally as big as the first, one wearing jeans, the other cargos.

Gabriel got to his feet and the guy in the jeans moved to take his shot. Katie was on him in a split second and grabbed his gun hand by the wrist, twisted it down, snapping it while delivering a kick to his knee and shattering his knee cap.

The guy in the cargos moved in and Gabriel dove at him, knocking him to the floor.

Ben wrestled with the big black guy.

Gabriel punched the guy in the cargos in the face, used to his powers giving him enough force to knock a guy out with one blow. When the guy didn't go under, he slammed his fist into the guy's face again. The man spat blood at him and threw him off to the side. Gabriel caught a glimpse of the unconscious form of the man in the jeans. Katie rolled off him then got in behind the man in the cargos and put him in a guillotine from behind. The way she had her hands positioned with the man's neck in the crook of her arm showed she was trained, and quite efficiently, too, as the man passed out quickly after she got her hands on him.

Ben slugged the big black guy and Katie came in behind him and brought her palms together in one swift blow to either side of his temples. The man crashed to the floor in a heap.

Two more guys emerged from the doorway—probably the ones who were on the lookout outside, Gabriel guessed—and shot Ben. Ben went down with a hole in his chest. It happened so fast Gabriel couldn't see precisely where he'd been hit or if he was dead already.

Katie kicked the gun out of the man's hand then delivered another kick square into the guy's solar plexus. Gabriel lunged forward and the man shot at him, just missing Gabriel's feet but causing enough of a jolt to make him stop advancing.

With another kick to the man's neck, which made a loud crack as his head lurched to the side, Katie dropped him, then was pistol-whipped by the other.

She spun around with the blow and came around, kicking him in the gut in what seemed like reflex. The man staggered back a step, but not before firing off another shot just as Katie raised his gun arm, forcing the shot to hit the ceiling.

Gabriel ran in, mad at himself for not acting as quickly as he should have or as quickly as he had in similar armed situations in the past. He suddenly realized how much he'd come to rely on his powers and without them activated, he was reacquainted with the fear of not having any advantage over anyone.

He plowed into the guy just as Katie twisted the gun free from the man's hand and shot him. The man fell down dead and Gabriel grabbed her by the shoulders only to have her arms come up in between his and her palms shoot out to throw his grip off her. She kicked him in the chest, sent him to the ground, the gun aimed at him. The look in her eyes showed she was cold and distant, a soldier, programmed to kill.

He raised his hands. "Katie, please, don't do this." He wasn't pleading for his life. He was pleading for hers.

Her blue eyes remained cool and fixed on his.

Chest aching from the kick, he said, "Put the gun down."

She grimaced—then her expression softened, as if she had suddenly changed into somebody else. With a slight shake of her head, she lowered the weapon and stepped over to Ben, who had his hand on top of the bloody wound on the right side of his chest. He exhibited quick, shallow breaths.

Katie knelt at his side and put her hand on his, then, with a frown, pressed his hand down on the wound with so much force he cried out. She brought the barrel of the gun to his head.

"What are you doing?" Gabriel shouted.

She ignored him and instead asked Ben, "Where were you supposed to meet up after here?"

Ben's glazed-over eyes were barely visible through his mostly-closed eyelids, but Gabriel could tell he was looking at her. "I already told you, before, way back earlier."

"You're lying," she said, and put even more pressure on his hand. He tried to swat at her with his free arm, but she knocked his hand away with the butt of the gun. By the way the metal struck the bone, Gabriel could only guess how much it hurt.

"I'm not lying, I swear," Ben said through gasping breaths.

Katie released the pressure off his hand.

"Back off him," Gabriel said and came down beside her. He put his hands on her shoulders, about to pull her away.

She shrugged him off. "I know what I'm doing."

"So do I," Gabriel said.

Katie elbowed him in the nose and the warmth of blood immediately gushed over his lips and down his chin. He pulled up the collar of his shirt to catch as much as he could lest whoever investigated this scene found it once they were gone.

When she looked at him, he could see in her eyes she knew she'd found a weak spot: paranoia of discovery.

Hope she doesn't figure out what I'm trying to keep hidden, he thought.

Katie pressed down on Ben's hand, this time curling his fingers inward so they dug into the wound. "The drop-off, Ben. Spare me the lies. You're going to die and unless you want that stuff to fall into the wrong hands, at least let me go get it."

When Ben spoke, his words were raspy and strained. "If I'm . . . not there . . . they'll . . . they won't give it to anybody . . . to anybody else."

"Place and time. I know it was this morning. Give me specifics," she said and pressed down harder on his hand.

Gabriel eyed the gun in her hand, which was pressed up tight against Ben's temple. He saw her finger locked taut on the trigger. If he tried to redirect the barrel, she was clearly too fast a person and would most likely squeeze off a round before it pointed elsewhere. Ben would certainly be dead and he couldn't have that.

"Let's go, Katie," he said.

"Not until he talks."

Ben's breathing came on quick and he coughed up spurts of blood.

Katie pressed his hand into the wound with everything she had. Ben cried out.

"Tireland Warehouse on King," he said.

"When?"

"Tire . . . Tireland on . . . on . . ." Ben went limp and a slow wet wheeze escaped his throat.

Katie kept her hand on the trigger, the gun to his temple.

Let it go, Katie, Gabriel thought. He needed her to release the weapon. She didn't, but did pull it away from Ben's head.

She turned to Gabriel and said, "You should've stopped me. I guess you're not who I thought you were."

CHAPTER TEN

KATIE EXPLAINED SHE'D keep the gun with her prints on it until they were by the river, then she'd dump it. As they walked, Gabriel listened as she explained who Ben really was: nephew to the city's most powerful crime boss, Andrei Aleksei. Ben had been both a drug runner and dealer, with special areas of interest in weapons and human trafficking. He had set his sights on Katie to force her into one of the city's main prostitution rings, but when he tried to do so by force, she quickly showed him she would have none of it and broke two of his fingers.

"Why'd you stay with him?" Gabriel asked her as they walked down Higgins.

"I didn't 'stay' with him. I told you before he and I were never an item. But I stuck around him and strung him along because of who he's connected to. Even when he wanted to take me out because of what I did to him, I persuaded him otherwise. Found his soft side and used it to my advantage. I caught wind a big exchange was going down with Ben being one of the central players. What do you think tonight was all about? Just some regular ol' street drugs?"

"Thought it might've been a gang war."

"A gang war? Oh please. You're so naïve. Guys from opposite sides plug each other all the time. They fight all the time. They utter threats all the time. If you call that 'war,' then fine, but tonight started with Tee-lo. They knew he'd talk about whatever Ben had told him about the deal, so they beat it out of him then sent him to Ben as a message they had power over one of his guys and for Ben and his crew to back off when things went down."

"Which is when?"

"This morning sometime. You were there, Mike. Ben died before I could get the exact time out of him."

"At least we got the location."

"It's a start."

Gabriel's nose had stopped bleeding, but the blood had soaked right through his shirt and to his uniform beneath. If he had to change into Axiom-man again, the stain would be there and if Katie saw him, she'd put two and two together in a hot minute. "I still don't understand why you're involved in all this or why now you're not simply going home."

"I can't let this deal go through. There's something too valuable at stake and" —she stopped walking and faced him— "I can't let the wrong people get control of it."

Gabriel stopped and faced her. "Of what, Katie? What is it you're not telling me?"

"It's a weapon," she said. "A very powerful one. If Ben had gotten ahold of it, him and anyone else, including Aleksei, would be unstoppable."

"Why don't you just go to the police, tell them what you know?"

"I can't go to the police. You saw what I did tonight. They can't know I was involved. Besides" —she glanced off to somewhere past them— "the other bad guys *are* the police."

CHAPTER ELEVEN

6:30 A.M. - OUTSIDE, GOING TO TIRELAND

THE NEWS SHOOK Gabriel to the core. The cops? How could they be involved? "I'm sorry, but you must be mistaken. How could the police have anything to do with this?"

She slightly squinted her eyes. "You really are that clueless, aren't you? I would've expected more. Aleksei is paid up with all the right people in the municipal government, provincial, federal—including Winnipeg's Finest. You get guys working for him who are supposedly on the right side of the law running around with this weapon and this city is going to fall apart and there'll be nothing anyone can do about it." She looked him square in the eyes. "Not even Axiom-man."

The way she said it made her sound like she'd lost all faith in Axiom-man's capabilities. After tonight, after the display of fear, uncertainty under duress—even *he* was disappointed in Axiom-man. His going undercover, being "Mike" and tasting the city's underworld was meant to help him grow as a hero, bring to light parts of the criminal structure he'd never seen before. Now he was in the thick of it and was dismayed at his own limitations as exemplified this night. Without his powers—he felt like he did before the messenger visited him all that time ago, before the costume, before the decision to use his abilities for good.

He felt worthless.

He couldn't feel that way any longer. There wasn't a place for that in his life. There couldn't be. It was having those kinds of holes in his armor that contributed to the chaos of the past night and hindered his ability to have taken care of business as quickly and efficiently as he should have. No more. If being "Mike" was part of taking his crusade as Axiom-man to the next level, then he was going to see it through. This city needed him, and it needed a more well-rounded him, and not just someone who relied solely on superpowers and a costume to get things done.

It was time to bring in elements outside of the flight, the ultra strength, the eye beams.

"If we can't go to the cops," Gabriel said, "then we do this ourselves." *I hope.*

"Fine, but we do it my way, and I need you to promise me something."

"What?"

"If things get crazy, if our back's against the wall, you have to promise me you'll do what needs to be done to finish this."

"I won't kill anyone, Katie." *I promised myself that recently. I'll never take a life again.* "But I'll see this through."

Her expression was like steel. He'd never seen that in a girl before. What could've possibly happened to her that would've set her on this path?

"Tireland's not far from here," she said. "They'll have watchdogs everywhere."

"Then how are we going to get in?" he asked.

"Simple," she said. "You're going to go in the front door."

———

7:12 A.M. - NOT FAR FROM TIRELAND

Gabriel and Katie had arrived in the area about twenty minutes ago, so hung around the perimeter and kept out of sight until they saw morning traffic start to kick in. A few civilians walked up and down the streets, others waiting on buses, thus making it easier to make their way closer to the building undetected from any surveillance.

"Keep your eyes peeled," Katie said. "These people you see, they might not be who they seem."

When they were two streets over was when they would split off.

In an alleyway, inside one of the doorways, Katie drew Gabriel in close. Immediately, his guard went up and he felt a wall rise in his heart. She put her arms around him, brought him in tight and drew his head down beside hers. It took a second, but he realized she was doing this so any onlookers would think they were just an amorous couple walking it off after a wild night and couldn't help themselves but sneak off for one last "goodbye." She smelled good, even after a night of fighting. Her body—small but strong, yet soft to hold—reminded him of Valerie's. He felt like he was betraying her.

"Thanks for doing this," Katie said. "Stick to the plan. That's the most important thing you can possibly do in situations like these. I'm relying on you to hold up your end. I'll keep up mine."

Except, Katie hadn't told him all of what her end entailed.

"What we do this morning is important on all fronts," she said. "It's for the good of this city, both presently and later. It's also" —her voice dropped to a whisper— "for myself. There's one more thing I need to do."

"Anything I can help with?"

"Just let me do it."

He didn't quite get it, but this mission seemed to mean a great deal to her and not simply on a moral level. Something deep ran through her regarding this. Who would've thought the small blonde playing pool earlier would've led him on such an adventure, giving him everything he wanted when he set out to see the ugly side of the city?

"Stay safe," she told him.

"You, too."

She didn't hug him, but instead pushed him away and nodded toward the mouth of the alley, making it clear she wanted him to get going.

Stuffing his hands in his pockets, Gabriel gave her a final nod then headed to Tireland.

He kept to the sidewalk as planned, head low, feigning he was one of the many off to work this morning. Once again he thought how he'd have to be at the office in about an hour and a half and how most likely that wasn't going to happen. He forced himself to keep his mind focused on the task at hand when he started thinking of how he was going to ask his folks for money if he couldn't find a replacement job in time, and there was no way he was going to move back home. Not now, not after becoming Axiom-man. He needed the freedom and his parents weren't exactly the type to let him do whatever he wanted, despite him being in his mid-twenties.

Coming up around the corner, Tireland a mere two sidewalk lengths away, Gabriel wished he had his sunglasses. He could power-up and be ready in case whoever he encountered tried to assault him. But that wasn't part of the plan. He kept transforming into Axiom-man as a contingency though, and if Katie figured out who he was, well, he'd deal with that later.

The notion of the cops being rolled up with Aleksei and his associates put a knot in his stomach. Did the police chief, Mark Henderson, know about this? Did Jack Gunn? Was Jack or Henderson one of them? Had he been dealing with crooked cops this whole time and didn't even know it?

Never had he felt so alone in his crusade. He thought he had the backing of the police if worse came to worse. Any stability and peace of mind that once offered had just been ripped out from under him.

If Katie was telling the truth, that was.

The old double doors leading into the Tireland warehouse came into view. A white delivery truck sat outside, but he doubted that was the truck that contained the weapon. Gabriel walked past it then up the warehouse's steps.

From behind him: "Can I help you?" A thin wiry guy with a mullet and mustache leaned his head out the truck's window.

"Yeah," Gabriel said. "I'm an independent contractor, specialize in playgrounds. Heard this place had a lot of leftovers from its heyday. Tires make great bedding for around junglegyms. Good for the kids' knees, no scrapes and all that. Was told I could come by and snoop around, maybe take inventory then come back and take a pile of them off your—well, maybe not *your* hands—but lighten the load in there." It was meant to be unbelievable.

The guy stared at him as if truly weighing his story.

"Right," the guy said. He stepped out of the truck and stood taller than Gabriel first guessed. He was probably six-five, six-six. The man wore light blue overalls.

"Think you could help me out?" Gabriel asked.

The guy came up to him and looked up and down the sidewalk before settling his gaze on him. Another guy came out of the back of the truck, this one shorter, but still as lanky. He wore similar faded blue overalls.

"Right this way," the man said and walked past Gabriel to the front door.

He bought it. Whatever. Gets me— A sharp pain spiked at the base of his skull and the lights went out.

Chapter Twelve

TIME UNKNOWN - INSIDE THE WAREHOUSE

THE HAZY IMAGE of a guy with a wide shaved head slowly faded into view. The two guys in overalls were to the left of the man. The back of Gabriel's head ached right down his neck and all across his shoulders. His stomach swam, so much so he had to clench his fists to keep from throwing up. The bones around his eye sockets hurt as well as the bridge of his nose. He could only assume these guys had some fun with him while he was out. His hands were bound behind him and he was on a hard metal chair. Being tied up was something that had been happening to him a lot lately, the last of which was being bound in a cave while werewolves constructed a sacred rite just outside it.

"He's coming around," the guy with the shaved head said.

"Think I should dust him one more time before Andrei gets here?" said the man with the mullet, who was immediately to his left.

"By all means."

The man's fist came flying in from the side. The last thing Gabriel saw was the sight of his own knee as white pain lit up the side of his head.

TIME UNKNOWN - THE DARK

Voices spoke somewhere on the other side of the darkness. Gabriel knew he had his eyes closed, but try as he might, he couldn't open them. His head spun and he felt like he was falling backward but never hitting the ground. The only comfort he had was knowing he wasn't alone, that someone—he couldn't remember who—was out there looking out for him. He thought he could break free out of the darkness if he turned something on, but wasn't sure what that thing was. A switch? A feeling? Did he have to say something or ask someone?

The voices were muffled as they filtered through the ringing in his head and the ache in his ears. Gabriel wasn't sure, but he thought he felt something wet leaking out of his ears as well.

"Who's he?" The voice was low, matter-of-fact.

"Some guy snooping outside."

"Don't know him?"

"Do you?"

"If I did, I wouldn't have asked who he was, now, wouldn't I?"

Another voice, real deep. "Think we should pop him and call it good."

"Kill him, and you might mess the whole thing up." The matter-of-fact guy again.

"He's just a schlub, man, come on. Nobody's going to miss him."

"Don't you think it's strange that we're about to do this thing and we got someone coming up to this place after nobody has for weeks 'cept our guys?"

"Could be one of those bad-place-bad-time things."

"Or you could be a moron, which I'm betting on. I'm thinking" —the man's voice suddenly got louder and

Gabriel felt hot air on his face— "he's wired or wearing some sort of surveillance gig." The voice went quieter and the hot air stopped. "You know, to check things out."

"Why'd they do that?"

"Do I look like a cop? I don't know. He's probably one of them, but they forgot the deal: only those in the know get to come in."

"So we shouldn't've brought him in?"

"You should've just hustled him along outside but now you bring a guy in here, knock him around a bit, and . . . . You can't let him back outside!"

The men exchanged a few other words, but the last ones rang loud and clear: "Give me your gun."

A shot sent a jolt through Gabriel's system and his heart hit overdrive. Violent pain hit his abdomen. The darkness remained and he fell backward, but his brain was coming around now, perhaps from the rapid rush of blood circulating his system. Something hard hit him in the back as his brain finally came around and he was able to think straight again.

Rafter beams and wide metal vents faded into view.

Gunfire sounded all around him.

He couldn't breathe.

The pain in his gut was now in his chest. Through hazy vision, he looked down at his body, expecting to see his chest blown wide open and blood gushing everywhere from where the bullet struck.

Except . . . there was no blood, only a body in overalls on top of him. One of the men from earlier, the guy with the mullet.

Confused, Gabriel shuffled his weight beneath the man, the echoing of gunfire making his heart skip a beat with each shot.

The room came into better focus, though the puffy flesh around his eyes created a dark halo around his vision like he was looking through a pair of binoculars.

The guy was too heavy so Gabriel *shifted*, activating his powers and his ultra strength. He ripped the ropes binding his hands behind him with ease, brought his arms around, skin scraping along the warehouse's cement floor, then shoved the guy off of him. The man falling onto him had been the pain he experienced, not a gunshot wound.

Gabriel got to his feet and *shifted* his powers off. He quickly checked his clothes to make sure the men hadn't discovered his costume beneath. From what he could tell, everything was in order. That wasn't to say they didn't see something they shouldn't have and decided to keep that information to themselves, but there was no time to dwell on it.

Men—many more than had previously surrounded him when he was tied up—darted around the room, some popping up from behind old benches, others from behind shelving units and supply racks. A big desk was turned over on its side.

He had to get moving lest he get caught in the crossfire.

Gabriel found cover behind a large heap of tires. The scent of old rubber was overpowering and he made a conscious effort to breathe through his mouth to avoid the smell.

The plan had been for him to get caught and for whoever was inside to be preoccupied with him while Katie came in from elsewhere and liberated the weapon. He'd then try to talk his way out of the building or, if he had to use force, discreetly use his powers to get him out of there. Katie didn't know about the powers part, just that he would fight his way out and, if he couldn't hold his own, she'd join him and help him out. He didn't count on getting the tar beaten out of him and he didn't think Katie would start a gunfight. Somebody must've seen her and if they were still firing and shouting, he could only assume she was still alive and somewhere in the warehouse.

Gabriel peered over the mound of tires, thinking maybe there'd be a phone on the wall, then thought better of it because any communication capabilities this place had would've been disconnected long ago. So much for calling the police.

For now, *he* was the police.

And he had to think fast and help Katie.

He reached up to undo his shirt and change into his gear, but stopped when he realized that if Axiom-man showed up, it might scare Katie off and, potentially, take the weapon with her if she already had it. Whatever that weapon was, he couldn't let it fall off his radar. If it was so important that Katie was willing to lay her life on the line for it, and if it was going to be the subject of a deal between Winnipeg's Finest and Aleksei, then it had to be crucial.

But he needed an edge and so again activated his powers. He'd just keep his gaze away from anyone he encountered to avoid suspicion.

He got to his feet and, using his flight as an aid, scaled the warehouse shelving units until he was up in the rafters. From up here, he could see everything, including all the men—fourteen in total—firing their weapons.

Where was Katie? Every time a shot rang out and the men returned fire, Gabriel couldn't locate the source of the first shot. It had to be her though.

Men screamed and yelled as they were gunned down.

Gabriel ran across the beams, using his flight to keep in balance, and found a couple guys hiding on the far side of the room, weapons drawn and seemingly just waiting to unload. Gabriel dropped down behind them and grabbed each of them by their ears and slammed their heads together, knocking them out. He took a quick glance around to make sure no one was looking then flew back up into the rafters.

He crossed to the other side of the room where a couple of goons were hiding out behind a wide shelving unit that still had some tires on it. One was on either end. If he took out one, the other might see him so whatever he did, he had to act fast. He could've used his eye beams to zap the weapons from the men's hands, but it wouldn't knock them out and would only escalate the panic. His best bet was to neutralize the conflict by getting as many men unconscious as he could and hope Katie was able to do the same.

He dropped down to the top of the shelving unit and stood over the first guy at the end. Quickly, he landed behind him, bringing his arm down on the other side of the man's body so he could grab the hand with the gun. The guy squeezed the trigger the second Gabriel made contact and shot a hole in the cement. Gabriel squeezed the man's wrist, forcing him to drop the gun, then delivered a swift blow to the side of the man's head. The guy dropped. Gabriel spun around and grabbed a tire off the shelf just as the man on the other end caught sight of him. Gabriel hurled the tire at him at the same time the man let off a shot. The bullet missed and the tire struck the guy across the chest, knocking him down. Gabriel leaped into the air, landing on the guy and clocked him twice in the forehead. The man stopped moving.

Gabriel went back up into the rafters and still counted seven—he saw Katie run up behind a guy, jump over him and use the man's own gun against him—six men standing.

His heart ached; she had killed and no matter how this whole thing ended up, he'd have to take her in as a result even if what she was doing was considered self-defense.

Three guys were huddled together over by the pile of tires he had gone behind after he got free of his chair. Katie was sneaking up a shelving aisle one over from them, gun ready. He had to stop her. He made his way across the rafters then saw someone tailing her. The man stooped down by one of his fallen comrades and picked up the other guy's weapon. He aimed to shoot.

"No!" The word came out before Gabriel could think and he dove off the rafters and landed on the guy, deflecting his gun hand away. He punched him out just as a pile of shots rang out in the direction of the tire pile.

Gabriel ran over and took the tire pile in one leap. Only when he landed on the other side did he realize how foolish it was potentially jumping into the line of fire like that. Katie stood over the three men, smoke trickling out the barrel of her gun.

Gabriel turned away from her so she wouldn't see the blue glow over his eyes. He hoped she didn't notice his blue hair sticking out from under his hat. If he powered down in front of her, the shift in color might catch her attention. "What did you do?"

"What needed to be done. There's two more. One's in the office across the way. I lost the other one."

"Stay here."

"I don't think—"

"Stay. Here. Katie."

He checked over the tire pile to make sure the coast was clear then hopped over it, careful to go up and over it normally without the aid of flight.

The office door across the way was closed and the blinds to the window looking out over the plant were drawn. Doing his best to stay behind large objects, Gabriel kept his eyes peeled for the second man who was somewhere in the warehouse. Once he reached the office door, he sidled up against the wall and reached for the doorknob. He tested it as gently and quietly as possible. When it didn't turn over, he forced the lock, hearing the mechanism break inside the jamb. He shoved the door open and when no shots followed, he peeked around the corner to find the office empty.

She set me up. She even locked the door and closed it. He marvelled at her ability to plan one, two even three steps ahead. Where did she learn this stuff?

A shot echoed throughout the warehouse along with a man's yell. Assuming the guy was down, that left one more. Gabriel also hoped the men he knocked out didn't regain consciousness anytime soon.

He was about to fly up into the rafters again, but stopped when he heard Katie shriek. He ran in the direction of the sound and saw her face-to-face with the last of the men, a body by her feet.

"Please don't kill me," she said. "Please don't kill me." She started crying and shaking.

What's she doing? Gabriel thought.

The man across from her, who Gabriel recognized as the guy with the shaved head from earlier, seemed at a loss as to what to do. He stood, shuffling on his feet, gun aimed squarely at Katie.

"I beg you, please, let me go. I won't tell anyone what happened here, I swear. It wasn't even me. All you guys shot—"

"Shut up!" the man yelled. "I saw you kill Franco."

I'm not fast enough to take him out, Gabriel thought. *I rush in from the side, and he'll fire. If I shoot the gun or his hand with my eye beams, it'll give me away.* Maybe it was time to come clean and show Katie who he really was?

But there was one other choice.

Gabriel stepped into view. "Hey!" The man spun to face him, the gun, too. The shot went off and Gabriel's ribs lit up with pain just as Katie came and tackled the man from the side. Gabriel staggered back a step. Katie was on top of the guy and grabbed the hand holding the gun. The loud snap of bone told him she just broke the man's wrist. With a couple of strikes to the head, she put the guy out, then pressed the barrel of the gun to the man's forehead.

"Stop!" Gabriel shouted.

"No witnesses."

He *shifted* his powers off. "That's not how to do things. Look at how many lives you've already taken." He looked down at his ribs. The bullet grazed him. It was bleeding, but not gushing.

"They tried to kill me."

He swallowed the pain in his side. "Revenge isn't the answer."

"It is."

"You want justice, Katie. That's the answer. This man will pay once the police arrive."

"They're already outside. I saw them through the window as I was running past. Those men out there aren't going to be happy when they find the men in here."

"Then we'll leave."

"Not without the weapon."

"Then get it and we'll go together."

"We can't just walk out that door, Mike." She pressed the barrel of the gun even harder against the man's forehead.

"Put the gun down."

"It has my prints. I wasn't thinking. Still more to learn."

What was she training for? "Then don't use it against him." He couldn't believe he was going to say his next words. "Take it with you."

When he said that, she looked at him and her expression softened. Gabriel reached out his hand toward her. "Please, Katie, let's go."

She stared at the man, grimaced, then pushed herself off him. She stood over him and Gabriel carefully extended his hand toward the gun.

"No witnesses," she said and shot the guy anyway.

Gabriel grabbed the gun away from her with such force he pulled her away from the dead man. He was surprised how much she moved despite him not having his powers activated.

Her blue eyes were void of life and he wasn't sure who he was talking to anymore. What had happened to her that would set her on this path? Her skill set was unbelievable and her ability to kill without remorse unsettling.

"Find the weapon, then we go. I'll get us out of here," he said.

She held his gaze, the muscles in her face not flinching once at his command. She said, "They're here."

A loud bang echoed throughout the room as what sounded like the heavy main door to the place slammed open.

CHAPTER THIRTEEN

"HANDS IN THE air. Now!"

Gabriel and Katie immediately complied. Gabriel saw a flash of panic cut across Katie's face. It was the first time she'd genuinely showed weakness since he met her. After dealing with so many guns over the course of his career as Axiom-man, he was immune to the weapon's presence, so he raised his eyebrows and softened his expression in an effort to play along and, maybe, play possum as well.

"Who are you two? What are you doing here?" the man asked. He had black hair, neatly parted to the side from the right. He wore a black button-down and matching black dress pants. The men behind him dressed similarly, all tidy and clean-shaven. Their haircuts ranged from medium-length up top to a quarter-inch shaved, but all had short-groomed hair by the ears and collar.

Cops.

So Katie had been right. These men were going to deal with these guys on whatever this weapon was.

"Answer me!"

When Katie spoke, she took on a Russian accent. "My name iz Nadiya Dotsenko, Spetsnaz. Ve got teep ov sale of vepon. Came to see. Dis place iz zurrounded wit' snipers on ze roof vaiting for my signal."

If she's telling the truth, she did a great job of playing me all night, Gabriel thought. *But Spetsnaz? Really? Katie might be a lot of things, but a good liar she isn't. At least, for something of this magnitude.*

"Spetsnaz, huh?" the man in black said. "I don't think so. You're under arrest, kid."

"If I vasn't Spetsnaz, how vould I know your name iz Trent Miller, eight-year career officer, vife Isabelle, keedz Mark and Gavin. Your address iz—"

"Okay, enough!" He kept the gun poised. "You better produce some identification, lady."

She smirked. "Iz in other pants."

Officer Miller glanced down and for a second Gabriel saw the wheels turning behind the man's eyes. Things weren't going to plan and Miller had no idea how to react. Even the guys behind him seemed dazed over the issue. A couple of them glanced around at the bodies littering the floor.

Officer Miller looked back up again. To Gabriel he said, "What about you? What's your story?" Miller glanced over his shoulder and gave a nod to one of his guys, who nodded back then turned and left.

Before Gabriel could speak, Katie spoke for him. "This iz Yuri Reznikov. He's bodyguard. Does not speak English."

Gabriel pretended like he hadn't heard her and played along.

Miller inched closer, his gun inching closer with him.

"What in the blazes is going on here?" came a familiar voice.

The men in front of Gabriel and Katie parted and Jack Gunn, captain of the new Special Force Unit designed to combat and detain super-powered criminals like Redsaw, Bleaken—and even Axiom-man, if he got out of hand—stepped through. Jack was around five-eight, thick, with gray mixed in with his brown hair. He kept a short-trimmed beard, and was wearing his trademark brown leather overcoat over a ratty white button-down.

Gabriel clenched his teeth, trying not to show reaction. Jack? He was supposed to be an ally. Was he dirty like these guys? This whole time? Recently? Did someone back him into a wall after the formation of the new unit and buy him out? Or were the cops in front of them actually the good guys and this whole thing was a sting operation meant to draw out whatever the Aleksei crime family was trafficking.

Jack pointed a stubby finger in Gabriel's face. "You better start talking. You're standing in a room full of dead guys."

"They're Spetsnaz, sir," Miller said. He leaned in close and whispered, "She knew my name, my history."

Jack simply grimaced. "She's not Spetsnaz, you idiot. She's a kid. Can't believe you'd even fall for that." Jack glanced around the room. "Cuff 'em and keep a weapon on 'em." He came right up to Gabriel and squinted his eyes as he scanned him over. Did Jack somehow recognize him? He could only imagine how terrible he looked with the swelling around his eyes.

A couple of officers came behind Gabriel and Katie, pulled their hands down, and put a pair of cuffs on them.

"You're going to walk us through what happened here," Jack said. "And with a mug like that, something *did* happen here."

Miller came up to Jack again and whispered, "We're still looking." Miller looked at Katie then at Gabriel.

"Search the bodies," Jack said.

That suggests the weapon is small, Gabriel thought. He kept his head facing forward but looked over at Katie. He couldn't read her. Her eyes seemed fixated on something across the room, her mind elsewhere though he doubted that was really the case. Was she seriously considering taking on the cops? At this close range? At the same time, she *had* stormed a police station and broke a suspect out of custody.

What about himself? He had on his uniform underneath his clothes.

Then Jack said the very words he feared: "Search them."

They can't find out I'm Axiom-man, Gabriel thought. He had hoped the firefights for the day would be over, but now he had no choice. He lowered his head and squeezed his eyes shut, ready to *shift* and power up, when the cop who'd been behind Katie choked on something. The guy next to him let out a yelp. Gabriel opened his eyes to see Katie behind one of the cops, her arms around his throat, the small link in the cuffs pressing against the man's trachea. The other guy was on the floor, holding his hands between his legs and writhing in pain. How she got the cuffs from behind her body to in front *and* got herself in behind the guy he had no idea. Did she have ultra speed or was she just highly trained? Gabriel couldn't help but be impressed.

"Stay back or I kill him!" Her accent was gone.

All the other men in the room raised their weapons.

Jack grabbed Gabriel and put a gun to him. "Touché, lady, but you kill him and I kill your friend here."

Was he serious? What kind of negotiating tactic was this?

Gabriel faked a bad Russian accent. "She tell trooth. I Spetsnaz." *Man, I suck.*

"Quiet!" Jack pressed the gun to Gabriel's head.

Jack was never the nicest kid on the block, and as Axiom-man, he and Jack barely saw eye-to-eye on anything. And if the guy *was* a bad seed, it would explain why he didn't like Axiom-man from the start.

"I'm serious!" Katie said. "Let him go or I break this guy's neck."

"Then you better get on with it, but not before you tell me where the weapon is," Jack said.

"Why don't you tell me?"

Gabriel still didn't know what this "weapon" was. Apparently it was small enough that it could've been on one of the men lying dead on the floor, but a couple of the officers that had gone searching for it were back with the group, guns aimed at them, and neither reported to Jack if they found anything.

As if Jack knew what Gabriel was thinking, he glanced back at his men behind him. The two officers that had gone searching for it shook their heads.

"I'm counting to three, kid, then this guy's gone."

Katie furrowed her brow and she looked Gabriel square in the eyes. He didn't know if she was weighing his life against her own or if she was trying to tell him something.

She held his gaze right until Jack said, "Count down starts now. Three . . . two . . . one."

Katie released the officer then gave him a violent kick forward, straight into Jack. When the men collided, Jack's grip on Gabriel's arm released.

Katie kicked the man on the floor, stole his gun, and opened fire.

Before Jack could reaffirm his hold on him, Gabriel ran over to Katie. Jack had his gun out. Katie aimed off to the side, fired and struck a propane can. A loud explosion shook the room as the thing went off. Some of the men froze. Others went flying. Anything wooden in the area caught fire immediately. The piles of tires started up and soon, Gabriel knew, the whole place would be filled with black smoke.

The propane can. So that's what Katie had been looking at across the room.

Using the explosion as a distraction, Gabriel powered up and snapped the cuffs behind his back. He grabbed Katie by the arm and firmly took her around a metal shelving unit and away from the cops, who seemed to have come back to reality and were shouting. A few advanced. Jack was lost in a giant plume of smoke.

The loud roar of flames rushed through the room and Gabriel pulled Katie away further.

He never made eye contact, not wanting her to see the blue glow behind his swollen eyes.

"We can't leave," she said. "We need to find it."

Gabriel had to shout over the roar of the flames. "What is it?"

"It's important."

"Cut the crap, Katie. Just tell me straight."

"I can't, Mike. It's too important." She moved to pull away from him but he only reaffixed his grip on her arm. He half-expected her to do some sort of maneuver that would get her away from him, but she didn't.

"You can't stay here."

"We have to find it." She put her hand to his face and nudged his jaw so he'd squarely look at her.

He resisted.

"Mike!" She tried again and before he could power down, she was looking into his eyes. "If we don't find it, there will be more people like you."

CHAPTER FOURTEEN

TIME UNKNOWN - INSIDE THE FIERY WAREHOUSE

A VIOLENT JOLT shook Gabriel's system.

Katie knew who he was.

He briefly considered saying he didn't know what she was talking about, but he was standing right in front of her with his eyes glowing and with blue hair, even if most of it was concealed by a baseball hat.

He didn't know what to say.

"Look, it's got to be somewhere close. Most of these guys will clear out of here. A few might remain. I know you're not invincible. If you want to help me, you need to get the men who remained out of here. Jack especially."

"What's his tie to all this?"

"The weapon is a means to make the ordinary extraordinary. They won't have super—"

She was cut off when a cop rounded the corner, spotted them, and opened fire. Gabriel shoved her out of the way and without even thinking zapped the gun from the man's hands with his eye beams. When he looked back to find Katie, she was gone.

"Katie!" he shouted.

Nothing but the roar of the ever-growing fire responded.

"Great," he said and rushed toward the officer.

"How did you—" the officer began.

"Quiet!" Gabriel punched him out, put the man over his shoulders, then immediately started looking for a way out. It appeared all exits on the ground level were blocked. The only option was to go up.

The room was quickly filling with toxic black smoke as the heaps of tires caught fire, and it was getting difficult to see.

"No choice," Gabriel said, and rose off the ground and headed for the first high-level window he saw. He shot a hole through it with his eye beams, the glass shattering. As quickly as possible, he flew the officer a safe distance away then took off into the air and went back inside the window into the warehouse. He landed on the ground and saw bodies burning. He didn't know if they were the men from earlier or the cops. They were too far along.

He ran up and down the aisles, leaping over fallen flaming debris when needed. Anybody that wasn't burning he knelt down beside and checked for a pulse. They were all dead.

"Katie!" he shouted.

The black smoke was so thick there was barely any light. He tried illuminating his eyes to see if that helped, but like back at the police station, it didn't fare so well against the smoke and only made it worse.

"Katie!"

He checked a few more aisles and saw the office, the one he had checked earlier but found empty. If there was a place to take cover in all this, it'd be there. He ran toward it then had to fly to the side when a pile of flaming tires fell into his path, blocking him.

He steeled himself and flew through the wall of flames, ignoring the heat as it pressed against him. When he landed on the other side, he patted at his clothes as best he could, thankful that he was wearing two layers and, if worse came to worse, he could always strip the outer one. He just wasn't sure he wanted Axiom-man at the scene here. Katie knew who he was, but anyone else who might be here didn't and while it'd make sense Axiom-man would come if he saw the place on fire, there was a chance—

Jack had Katie at gunpoint inside the office.

Gabriel reached the door. Katie looked in his direction. Jack took note and immediately turned to face him, gun poised. Katie rushed in from the side and the gun went off the moment she made contact with Jack. Gabriel moved out of reflex and was unharmed but a second shot went off as the two went down to the ground. Jack rolled Katie off him.

"No!" Gabriel shouted.

Jack went to aim at him and Gabriel blasted the gun from his hand.

"You!" Jack said.

Before Jack could reach for the gun, Gabriel grabbed him by the collar. "I should kill you for what you did." He couldn't believe he said it. It could've been the smoke, could've been the fatigue. Could've been Katie's body lying there. He didn't know.

His eyes glowed bright and fear filled Jack's face. Gabriel held his gaze . . . then brought the energy beams under restraint and didn't fire.

No. He wasn't a killer. He swore that was something he'd never do.

Katie lay off to the side. Her small body jerked when she coughed.

Gabriel dropped Jack and went over to her and rolled her over. "Thank God you're alive," he said. "We have to get out of here. The whole place will come down. Hang on." He scooped her up in his arms, stood and was tempted to walk past Jack. The very sight of the man made him sick. Not only was his once ally seemingly a dirty cop, but Jack had also pulled the trigger on a girl who was more of a hero than Jack would ever dream to be.

Maybe more of a hero than Gabriel himself would ever be . . . if heroes killed. That was where Katie went wrong and brought the word "hero" to shame.

But he couldn't leave him.

"Get up," Gabriel said.

Jack complied and Gabriel adjusted Katie and put her over one shoulder, held her tight, then grabbed Jack by his trench coat collar and lifted him off the ground. He didn't care if the weight of Jack's body against his coat hurt the man as the material cut into his arms. The guy deserved it.

He rose off the floor and headed toward the window and flew out.

He dropped Jack off a safe distance away from the building. Sirens rose not far from them and he knew the fire department and paramedics were on their way, but they were still at least five or six minutes out.

"I have to get you to a hospital," Gabriel said. He could get her there in less than two minutes.

"No, no hospitals," Katie said. "It's okay. I did what we needed to do. I got it."

"Where is it?"

"Take me away from here," she said. "They can't see it."

He complied and flew her to a nearby alley and laid her on the ground. When he stretched her out, he could see the blood on her shirt near her hips. Looked like the upper section of the femoral artery had been hit, which meant she'd bleed out within a few minutes.

He reached for the top of her jeans so he could peel them down and cauterize the wound. It could buy her some time.

"Leave it," she said. "This is more—"

"Put her down!" Jack was re-armed and at the mouth of the alley, gun drawn on them. He breathed heavily from sprinting over.

"She's dying!" Gabriel shouted.

"Axiom-man," Katie said and shifted her weight as she pulled a large metallic vial from her pants pocket. "Take this." She gave it to him.

The container held a vibrant blue liquid.

"It was in a safe in the office. Jack had the key, probably stage two of the pickup. Don't know what he was going to use it for."

"Put it down now!" Jack said and fired a warning shot off the brick of the nearest building.

Gabriel eyed the metal vial then fried it with his eye beams. The liquid inside began to boil and he dropped the container when it got too hot to hold. It smashed against the ground and he finished it off by melting it, the metal and the liquid mixing together.

Jack ran up, saw the melted mess on the ground, then went to swing at Gabriel. Gabriel blocked the punch and delivered one of his own, taking Jack out.

"Axiom-man?" Katie said, her voice weak and distant. She arched her back.

He picked her up in his arms. "I'm going to get you help."

"It's too late. But it's okay. It's the final step. It had to be done."

He didn't know what she was talking about and assumed she wasn't thinking clearly because she was dying.

"No, Katie. I'm going to get you help," he said.

"You did. You did help me," she said. "Thanks for—" She wheezed and went limp in his arms.

With a cry, Gabriel flew into the sky and took her body to the nearest hospital.

CHAPTER FIFTEEN

AXIOM-MAN CHECKED IN with the clerk and specified he wanted to see the body of who was identified as Katianna White.

"I'm sorry, sir, but I can't allow you in," the clerk, a small Filipino woman, said. "The hospital is under strict orders from the police to not allow you access."

Axiom-man was surprised Jack would even set up such an enforcement, but after clocking him in that alley, it made sense. He'd need to avoid Jack for a good while after this. "You have to. It's important." He needed to see Katie one last time and properly say good-bye. He hoped his clout as Axiom-man would get him what he wanted. Bottom line was he couldn't show up at the girl's funeral whether in costume or out. Jack would probably order a police presence for it and he would cause a ruckus if he saw Axiom-man there. Even if he went as Gabriel Garrison, there was the chance he might be recognized and he couldn't have Jack know his secret identity if Jack somehow saw past the glasses, different demeanor and what would hopefully be by then a face that wasn't swollen from taking a beating.

The woman at the counter said, "I was told no admittance to anyone, but you help people so I make an exception but" —she leaned in close— "there is a policeman by the door, so he won't let us."

"Leave him to me," Axiom-man said.

The woman led him down a plain hallway to the last room. When the cop standing outside the door saw him, he reached for the radio on his shoulder.

"Wait," Axiom-man said.

The man paused.

"I know you have loyalties," Axiom-man said, "but I need to go in there."

The guy seemed confused and quickly gave himself away as a rookie by saying, "I'm under orders to . . . I mean—"

"Look, I won't say anything if it ever comes up, Officer" —he checked his nameplate— "Turner."

Turner took a deep breath then nodded. "I'm coming in with you or no access. I'm sorry."

The rookie had more guts than Axiom-man gave him credit for and now wasn't the time to enforce his will on the officer.

"Fine," Axiom-man said.

The three went in and the clerk went to the mortuary refrigerator, which was stacked four cubbies high and five wide.

She checked the labelling on the square doors and said, "This one."

She opened the small door and pulled out an empty gurney.

11:28 P.M. - OUTSIDE DAVE'S BAR

Axiom-man stood on the rooftop across the street from Dave's Bar. A few people lingered around outside, having a smoke and minding their own.

He didn't know why he was here, exactly. Maybe a part of him half-expected Katie to show up. He tried to remember if he had seen her at Dave's before last night, but wasn't sure despite having tried to memorize faces. Dave's Bar was where it all began, though. In his effort to keep an ear to the ground, he ended up hearing—and finding out—a lot more than he was ready for.

Someone out there had developed the means to give people special abilities. Whether that meant genuine superpowers or something else, he didn't know. But Katie was right that that sort of power couldn't fall into the wrong hands. Axiom-man had already experienced as much when dealing with Redsaw and Bleaken in the past, never mind the other monsters he'd had to face in his career as a superhero.

But Katie. Shrouded in mystery and now missing.

A young girl who—

"I knew I'd find you here."

—was always full of surprises.

Axiom-man turned to face her. She stood about midway across the rooftop clad in a black hoodie, hood up, and black track pants.

"How are you still alive?" Axiom-man asked. "The truth."

"It was a superficial wound. It only looked worse because I made it bleed more than it should've. I'm fine, by the way."

"You died, Katie."

"I slowed my heart rate. A little trick I picked up along the way."

"How could you let me think you were dead?"

She took a step closer. "You weren't exactly honest with me, either. 'Mike,' is it? As if that would be your real name and, no, I don't expect you to tell me."

"I'm not going to." He crossed his arms. "Who are you? How could you do those things you did?"

She came close to him and looked out over Dave's Bar. He did the same. "It's all because of you, you know?"

"Me?"

"Kind of. It goes beyond that and the path I chose started before you came along, but you did show me the power of one person making a difference. You were the first to step up—to dramatically step up—and when I first saw you, I knew I had to follow suit, so I intensified my preparation."

"You mean you want to someday put on a costume and, what, fight crime?"

"The world's changing. You know that better than most. However, there are a lot of people out there who don't see that and view you, Redsaw, Bleaken and all the other weird things as just random occurrences, special circumstances or people. I know that's not the case and I know you're involved with something bigger than all this, than all of us."

She was perceptive. Though he didn't say it, she was talking about the inevitable battle to come between him and Redsaw, perhaps even the battle between the messenger and Redsaw's master.

"The police will be looking for you," he told her. "I don't think you thought it through, faking your own death."

"Maybe not, but it had to be done. This is what I want with my life and I had to lose myself to find myself. It was the final test in letting go and focusing solely on the task at hand."

"You killed people. I can't let that go unanswered for. You know that."

"Don't try to stop me. You can't."

"You're not unbeatable."

"I have to be."

"Why?"

She didn't answer.

"What aren't you telling me?" he asked. "What else do you know?"

"That wasn't the only vial containing the Enhancer—it's what they call it—there is more out there. It can't be used."

"How do you know this?"

"I make it my business to know."

"How?"

"Shut up and listen. That whole thing in the warehouse, me pretending to be Russian Spetsnaz, it might've been lame, but the point behind it was because the Enhancer was developed by the Russians. Jack Gunn caught wind of it thanks to his new intelligence hook up and set up a deal to acquire it. He's not dirty, so far as I know. But the cops with him were. It was a giant sting operation to get them out in the open that went horribly wrong and was a lesson to me in better planning. The Russians thought they were selling it to the Aleksei family hence Ben's involvement. The cops, the dirty ones, played Ben, making him think they were working for his uncle."

"Sounds complicated."

"These things always are." She took a slow breath, bit her lower lip. "At the same time, I think Jack wanted the Enhancer for himself. Maybe not necessarily for his own use, but for those of his choosing. He's been tasked with taking down super-powered threats, including you, if you ever go rogue. The City has Jack on a very tight leash and despite all his bravado, he has to answer to others much higher up on the chain. The Enhancer could give him or proper, good men an advantage over even the most skilled of criminals."

"What does it do?"

"It transforms a person into not only a perfect human specimen, enhancing speed, strength, stamina and every other athletic attribute, but it also reconfigures a person's DNA via genetic modification. That's where it gets tricky. I don't know what the modification is."

"You just said it makes a person a kind of super person."

"The modification is something else. I know taking attributes from different animals and insects is part of it, but what the result is, I don't know. There is also rumor of a supernatural source. I don't have access to that information. Yet."

"Why didn't you keep it for yourself?"

"For the reason I told you. I don't know what else it does and I'm not willing to take that risk. At least, not yet. The main objective is to ensure it doesn't fall into enemy hands."

"Seems it's already too late for that."

"The men from the warehouse? They didn't know what they had. They thought they were trafficking a chemical weapon, one the Alekseis could use discreetly when someone double crossed them. Those dirty cops thought Jack was on the take, too. They would've gotten it from Ben and used it for themselves, that is, in their minds a chemical weapon to perhaps manipulate those who have control over them, maybe even turn the tables. Hard to say for sure. Jack was the only one who knew what it really was, and the fact that Jack seemingly went ahead with the operation without Ben shows how important it is."

"Who's the main power players?"

"I'm not sure, but I can tell you that if you thought your little crime fighting backyard was just this city or maybe a place or two beyond, I can assure you that's no longer the case. This battle of yours has gone global." She turned to face him. "You need me."

He ran the information over in his head. Katie was right. He couldn't turn her in, not with the Enhancer still out there and, it seemed, with her having a few leads on how to track it down. Either everything she just told him was a lie and he was falling for it, or she was telling the truth. Yet, if she were blowing smoke, why would she meet him on this rooftop when she could just have easily disappeared?

He had no choice but to trust her, even at an arm's length. "Where will you go from here?"

"The less you know, the better." She put a hand on his shoulder. "Remember what I told you about Jack. He might be clean, but he's part of something big and you can't trust him completely. Don't tell him about me, everything I've just told you about the Enhancer, what you know about the sting at the warehouse—nothing."

"Okay." *I guess.*

She leaned in and hugged him, which took him off guard. He returned the embrace but only lightly as there wasn't anything behind it other than concern.

"Be careful," he said.

"You, too." She pulled away and took a step back. "I'll be in touch."

Shouts arose on the street below, capturing Axiomman's attention. He looked out onto the street in front of Dave's Bar. A couple of guys started shoving each other and one of them had a knife. It was time to go to work. When he looked up to say good-bye to Katie, she was already gone.

"Stay safe," he said, then dove off the rooftop to the fight below, remembering to do the same.

About the Author

A.P. Fuchs is the author of many novels and short stories. His most recent books are *Axiom-man: Outlaw; Axiom-man: Episode No. 2: Underground Crusade; Getting Down and Digital: How to Self-publish Your Book; Look, Up on the Screen! The Big Book of Superhero Movie Reviews; Canadian Scribbler: Collected Letters of an Underground Writer*, and *Redemption of the Dead*, the third book in his time travel zombie trilogy.

Also a cartoonist, he is known for his superhero series, *The Axiom-man Saga*, both in novel and comic book format. Please see **www.axiom-man.com** for more on this series.

Fuchs's main website is **www.canisterx.com**

THE AXIOM-MAN™ SAGA

AN ONGOING SUPERHERO BOOK SERIES
BY A.P. FUCHS

Available in paperback and eBook
at your favorite online retailer like Amazon.com